'Are your eyelashes real?' asked Ruth, softly.

'Everybody says they'd look better on a girl.'

'I think they look very nice on you.'

He turned to face her and she touched his eyelashes gently.

David was close enough to smell her perfume and he forgot all about the drink that he had been after. He had somehow known that this moment would arrive and he was re[illegible]

'Hel[illegible]

'Hel[illegible]

'Wh[illegible]

She [illegible]

'Ca[illegible]

Rut[illegible] er mind.

'Yes,' [illegible]

KENNETH HARPER

Dance With A Stranger

Based on an original film script by
Shelagh Delaney

PANTHER
Granada Publishing

Panther Books
Granada Publishing Ltd
8 Grafton Street, London W1X 3LA

First published by Panther Books 1985

A Panther Original

Based on an original film script by Shelagh Delaney

ISBN 0-586-06601-2

Printed and bound in Great Britain by
Collins, Glasgow

Set in Times

If you'll pardon the question,
It's a lovely suggestion,
Would you dance with a stranger
If the stranger were me?

1

London, Spring 1954

Knightsbridge lay cold and silent beneath a dark and hostile sky. Poised and elegant in their expensive winter fashions, the models in the shop windows looked out through sightless eyes at empty streets that were swept by an insistent breeze. A large black cat loped soundlessly along the pavement, its ears pricked, its tail erect. Sensing danger, it froze for a second, listened intently, then darted off into the shadows. It reached safety only just in time.

Out of the night came an explosion of noise and colour.

With rasping engines and raking headlights, a cluster of sports cars tore along the road as if it were a race track. They battled for the lead, took frightening risks, tempted fate time and again. The drivers were professionals out on a spree, handling their vehicles with an expert skill and daredevil confidence that had their female passengers screaming in excitement. When one car surged to the front and zigzagged crazily to keep the others at bay, a second machine mounted the pavement in order to overtake and almost collided with a lamppost as it rejoined the road. A symphony of horns acknowledged the new leader then the chase continued in earnest.

In the middle of the pack, at once part of the race and separate from it, was a gleaming Ford Zephyr Zodiac. Beside the other, smaller cars it looked flashily American with its chrome bumpers and trim, its white-edged tyres, its battery of lights and its spotless two-tone bodywork. Crouched behind its driving wheel was a short, stocky man with dark hair sleeked neatly back with Brylcreem and a pencil-thin moustache arching over a wide mouth. Unlike the other drivers, he was alone in his car. Unlike them, he mixed caution with boldness.

The leader now swung off the main road and took his pursuers through a maze of streets. Brakes squealed and tyres skidded as the vehicles tried to negotiate sharp corners at speed. Gear changes added jarring new notes to the general cacophony. Eventually, after a final spurt, they slowed right down to turn into the Brompton Road. Fanning out, they sought parking spaces beside both kerbs.

Doors slammed, voices were raised, laughter dominated. By the time that Desmond Cussen got out of the Zephyr and locked it behind him, the others had linked arms and were moving happily along the pavement as a single unit. They were the Beautiful People enjoying a night on the town, fun-loving extroverts on a voyage of discovery.

Desmond hurried to catch them up. He was older, quieter, more serious, better dressed than the others. Almost alone of the men, he was not a racing driver. He was a private man caught up in a group. An outsider with a desperate need to belong.

'Here we are!' he called.

The revellers stopped outside a handbag shop and some raucous jeers went up. From the window above, faint sounds of dance music could be heard. A discreet neon sign told them that they were at the Little Club. Desmond pushed his way to the front and rang the bell on the side door.

'Is Desmond really a member of the Little Club?' whispered a female voice.

'Yes!' hissed the man next to her. 'It's because he has such a little member.'

The Beautiful People hooted and sniggered. Not realizing that he was being laughed at, Desmond gave a thin-lipped smile. An eye appraised them through a peephole then the door swung open. Nodding to the man who had admitted them, Desmond led his friends inside. Pink wall lighting set off the deeper pink of the staircarpet. The music was louder now and was supported by a contented murmur of voices. Followed by the others, Desmond trotted up the stairs to be met at the top by the club receptionist, an oily young man standing behind a desk. He glanced over Desmond's shoulder.

'Guests of yours, Mr Cussen?'

'Yes.'

'If you'd care to sign them in, please, sir . . .'

Desmond took the proffered fountain pen and wrote neatly in the Visitors' Book. As they waited impatiently behind him, the women supplied giggles of anticipation and the men gave grunts of approval. When the newcomers had been duly signed in, Desmond waved them through to the club itself, savouring his moment of importance in the group. With muttered thanks, they filed past him.

The Little Club did not belie its name. It was effectively one small room into which tables, chairs and a well-stocked bar had been crammed. There was a space for dancing and a few couples were circling gently to the strains of a waltz that was being played on a gramophone. The club was new and had a vulgar opulence about it. Dark rose lighting bathed the whole place in a subdued glow. A pall of cigarette smoke suggested that the club had been busy all night.

As a dozen or more new faces came into the room, the customers turned to look at them. An amalgam of shock, surprise, embarrassment, curiosity and nervousness made the Beautiful People stop in their tracks. They took in their surroundings. They imbibed the atmosphere.

'Good evening, Mr Cussen . . .'

The spell was broken by the barmaid, a bird of paradise with heavy make-up and a welcoming smile. Desmond drifted to the bar and the others joined him. Drinks were ordered and the newcomers were soon relaxing and joking and starting to enjoy themselves. Most of them went off to find empty seats and Desmond was left at the bar with two of the men. He exchanged a few pleasantries with Christine, the vivacious barmaid, then he downed his whisky in a gulp and asked for another. Christine reached for the bottle.

Ruth Ellis watched it all with wry amusement from a table on the other side of the room. Pert, slim, attractive and wearing a low-cut, tight-fitting dress that showed off her shapely figure, Ruth was the manageress of the club. She missed nothing. Still only in her late twenties, she had the shrewd and experienced gaze of a much older woman. That gaze now turned elsewhere.

'Be careful!'

The shriek came from Claudette, one of the club hostesses, who was sitting beside Ruth. To impress Claudette, a middle-aged man was dancing in time to the music with a full glass of wine on his head. The hostess shrieked again as the drink threatened to fall but Ruth was equal to the emergency. Rising swiftly from her seat, she grabbed the glass with a deft hand just before it fell. The man immediately sat down beside Claudette and grinned lecherously at her.

'Now will you come out to supper with me?'

The hostess traded a glance with Ruth then smiled indulgently at the customer. Ruth began to clear away the glasses on the table. Feeling that he had earned his reward, the man leered at Claudette and squeezed her thigh. He was delighted with what he found.

'You've got wonderfully solid thighs,' he congratulated. 'How do you manage it?'

She raised a teasing eyebrow. 'I'm an acrobat.'

He chuckled lasciviously and moved in closer.

Ruth left them to it and headed for the bar. As she did so, she caught sight of the person standing beside Desmond Cussen. He was a tall, dark, dishevelled young man whose boyish good looks were marred by an arrogant scowl. His clothes looked as if they had been rescued from a jumble sale. He wore an old shirt, an old cashmere pullover, a jacket that was stained and creased all over, and a pair of baggy grey flannels. Around his neck was a woollen muffler that hung right down to his knees. Lounging insolently against the bar, he surveyed the room with a supercilious eye.

'You've brought us to a den of vice, Desmond,' he complained.

'You should feel at home then,' noted his other companion, a casually-dressed young man with a full moustache.

Ruth put the glasses on the counter as the first man spoke again. His tone of voice made her bridle at once.

'These places are glorified brothels.' He addressed the next graceless remark at Ruth. 'And who are you?'

'The glorified brothel-keeper,' she replied, levelly.

Desmond tried to introduce them to each other. 'David Blakely meet Ruth Ellis. She . . .'

But he got no further. Ignoring Ruth completely, David nudged his friend. 'You're a dark horse, Desmond. Isn't he?' he said, aiming the question at the other members of the group. 'I wouldn't have thought a sink of iniquity like this was his style!'

While Ruth had been glaring at David Blakely, the young man with the moustache had been studying her with fascination. He was mesmerized by the platinum blonde hair and the delicate features. He was drawn by her patent vitality. Beaming at her with frank admiration, he offered his hand.

'Cliff Davis . . .'

'Hello . . .'

They shook hands and his grin broadened.

'Will you dance with me?'

She sized him up for a moment then nodded her assent. Cliff led her to the dance floor with cavalier assurance and they began to waltz in time to the music. Ruth danced superbly, moving with graceful ease around the tiny space and capturing everyone's attention.

David Blakely sipped his drink.

'What did you say her name was, Desmond?'

'Ruth Ellis . . .'

Neither man could take his eyes off her.

Morris Conley was a big, balding, fleshy man of middle years who dressed with a spiv-like flamboyance. He had a smooth, plausible manner and a surface joviality that concealed a cynical hardness. A successful club owner with other flourishing business interests, Morris Conley kept a close watch on all his sources of income. As he sat behind a table in the flat above the Little Club, his practised fingers counted the week's takings. He was pleased with what he found and slipped an elastic band around the wad of notes before putting it back in the cash box.

Ruth Ellis watched him, a lighted cigarette between her fingers. She and her son lived rent-free in the well-appointed flat. It was one of the benefits of managing the club. There were times when she believed that it was the only benefit.

Conley gave her a flabby smile of satisfaction.

'Not bad, Ruth. Not bad at all.'

'I want a pianist,' she said, exhaling smoke.

'What's wrong with the record-player?'

'Nothing. But we should have both,' she argued. 'People like pianists. It'll pay off, Morrie. Don't be stingy.'

'You know me, Ruth. Part of the fun of having money is the pain of parting with it.'

'Do we get a pianist?'

While he considered the matter, he noted down the takings in his cash book. Ruth stubbed out her cigarette in an ashtray and stood directly in front of him.

'Well?'

'Why stop at a pianist?' he asked with an exaggerated shrug. 'We'll hire Harry Roy and his band, if you like. Or maybe you'd prefer Joe Loss?' He ran a podgy finger across his chin for a few moments then came to a decision. 'Give it a try.'

Encouraged by this one concession, Ruth went after another.

'And we should have book matches printed with the club's name. To give away. It's all publicity and it costs nothing.' She crossed to the mantelpiece and scooped up a couple of book matches. 'Look at these. The Clue Club . . . The Embassy . . . Everybody gives them away.'

'No,' he said, firmly.

'We're attracting a different class of customer now, Morrie.'

'They're all punters.'

'But . . .'

'The toffs like a bit of spit and sawdust.'

'Well, they're not getting it in my place,' she retorted.

'*My* place,' he corrected her. 'You manage it: I own it. And don't you ever forget that, Ruth.'

She bit back a reply and breathed in deeply through her nose.

Loud rhythmical noises came from the room above. On a cold February afternoon, one of the club hostesses was bringing some warmth and wonder into the life of a client. Judging by the sounds, he was determined to get his money's worth.

Trying to ignore it, Ruth poured two drinks and handed

one of them to her employer. Conley thanked her, took a sip, then gazed up at the ceiling with lewd interest.

'They're going at it a bit vigorous, aren't they?'

'I'm not planning to stay here for ever, Morrie,' she told him. 'I want to work for myself some day.'

'Don't cross the boss, Ruth,' he warned.

'I mean it.'

'So do I.'

He turned his head and looked her full in the face. The sounds from above had clearly aroused him. He raised a quizzical eyebrow at her. Ruth finished her drink and moved away to put her glass down on the mantelpiece. Conley appraised her through narrowed lids.

'Remember how we first met?'

'It was a lifetime ago!' she sighed.

'You were only a kid. Posing in the nude at the Camera Club. Giving those so-called "photographers" a cheap thrill.'

'I needed the money.'

'I showed you how to make a lot more, didn't I?'

'Yes, Morrie . . .'

'And you were grateful to me. Very grateful.' He ran a finger around the rim of his glass. 'You had a good body in those days, Ruth. You still have.' His voice took on a more coaxing tone. 'Go on. Order your book matches.'

'Thanks . . .'

He gazed upwards again and licked his lips.

'They'll bring the ceiling down at this rate.'

Anxious to deflect his lust, Ruth went quickly over to the radio and turned it on full blast. Then she yelled up at the ceiling.

'Shut up, you dirty devils!'

'Hey!' protested Conley. 'They're working.'

'Andrea will be home from school soon. I don't want him hearing that kind of thing.' Her employer laughed. 'I *don't*, Morrie!'

'If he's going to grow up in this place, he'd better start getting used to it.'

'He isn't going to grow up here!' she snapped.

'When the nobs want their nips out of the way,' he said with light sarcasm, 'they send 'em to Eton.'

She glared at him for an instant then found herself another cigarette. The noises from above continued with renewed force. Ruth began to feel that she was trapped.

David Blakely sat in a small office at the Hyde Park Hotel and stared at the clock on the wall. It was late evening and yet he still had an hour or more to wait before he came off duty. His stepfather had used his influence at the hotel to get David a job as a trainee catering manager but the latter had never tried to make a success of it. He found the work boring, his colleagues dull, and the unsocial hours a real handicap. There were so many more exciting ways to spend an evening.

He kicked open a drawer and took out a car magazine that he had hidden beneath a sheaf of papers. Flicking through the magazine, he came to a photograph of Cliff Davis, winning yet another race in the 1500 c.c. class. As he took the chequered flag, Cliff was giving a thumbs-up sign to the camera. David felt a surge of envy but it was not only prompted by his friend's achievement on the race track. He recalled the sight of Cliff Davis waltzing dreamily with the manageress of the Little Club. It was an image that David could not dismiss from his mind. He tossed the magazine back into the drawer and kicked it shut.

When he glanced up at the clock again, the minute hand did not seem to have moved at all. His patience ran out. Getting up from his chair, he smartened himself briefly then left the office. He went first to the dining room where he had a quiet word with the head waiter, then he walked through into the kitchen and made a show of speaking to the chefs. Since everybody seemed busy and preoccupied, he decided that he would not be missed.

Choosing his moment, he slipped out of the kitchen and sneaked out of the hotel by a side exit. When he had found his car, it took him barely more than a minute to drive across to the Little Club. He looked up at the neon sign and pondered. Then, without bothering to lock his car, he strode across the pavement and rang the bell.

Peggy Lee was revolving on the turntable, singing *Would you Dance With A Stranger*? In the middle of the dance floor, a couple were performing a gentle mambo. Ruth Ellis was dancing with her usual sensual grace, her long painted fingernails and her necklace catching the light as she moved. Desmond Cussen, her partner, was so lost in the magic of the moment that his eyes were shut tight. They cruised smoothly around until the record came to an end. Desmond blinked his eyes in disappointment.

'Let's go back to the table,' she suggested.

'After you . . .'

Desmond ushered her off the dance floor then held a chair for her to sit down. He took the seat opposite her and stared at her with a nervous intensity.

'Thanks for the dance, Ruth.'

'You're welcome.' She noticed her empty glass. 'I could do with another drink. How about you?'

'Yes, yes. Of course . . .'

Before he could get up, however, Christine came over to them with a tray. On it were two glasses and a bottle of champagne in an ice bucket. The barmaid unloaded the tray on to their table.

'With the compliments of the gentleman at the bar.'

Ruth put her glasses on so that she could see their benefactor more clearly. At the bar, leaning nonchalantly against the counter and wearing his smart, dark working suit, was David Blakely. He raised his glass to them and bowed his head slightly. Ruth was not impressed.

'Oh, it's that pompous little pillock friend of yours, Desmond!'

'Blakely!' grunted the other.

'Offensive little shit!' she said under her breath but she waved him over nevertheless and gave him a polite welcome. 'Do join us, Mr Blakely.'

'I will . . .'

He nodded to Desmond and sat down at the table. Christine went back to the bar and Ruth poured out champagne for all three of them. David was the first to pick up his glass.

'I hope this is the real thing,' he said, sceptically. 'The drinks are usually watered in these places.'

'Watered or half-inched, darling,' Ruth countered. 'Cheers!'

Before she drank, she fitted a cigarette into her long holder. Desmond, ever attentive, pulled out his lighter and held it against the end of her cigarette. Over the top of the naked flame, she watched David take his first sip of champagne. He seemed well pleased with it. She blew out smoke and then lifted her own glass. Both men clinked their own against it. Ruth had time for only the merest sip. The door opened and in streamed some more customers. She got to her feet automatically.

'Where are you going?' complained David.

'I must attend to my customers.'

'What about us?'

She left his question unanswered. Patting him on the shoulder, she glided across to welcome the newcomers and to make sure that they were soon ordering drinks. David and Desmond watched morosely until she disappeared from sight in the group of men clamouring around the bar. They could hear her laughing gaily at the ribald comments of some of her new guests. Evidently, she would not be returning to the table for a long time.

Desmond sighed and David helped himself to some more champagne. They exchanged a few desultory remarks but conversation only made them feel more uneasy. Two men who had never liked each other now had good reason for distrust and dislike. Both had sensed it the moment that they were together with Ruth. They were rivals.

The night wore on, the drink flowed, the music continued. Every so often the general high spirits would break out in an eruption of laughter or in some wild horseplay. Ruth circled the room tirelessly, sharing a joke here, joining in a game there, accepting invitations to dance from everywhere. When she finally repaired to the bar, Desmond seized the chance of going across to speak to her. Their chat did not last very long.

Out of the record-player came the distinctive voice of Edmundo Ros singing *I Came, I Saw, I Conga'd*. One of the club hostesses was immediately on her feet, earning a round of applause for the way that she swung her hips sensuously to the music. A pair of large male hands planted themselves on her waist and the conga was under way. The couple snaked between the tables to collect the other guests and the line got longer and louder. Desmond was in mid-sentence when he was grabbed by a hostess and incorporated into the dance. David was pulled from a chair, Ruth herself was drawn in, and Christine was hauled out from behind the bar.

The room was a cauldron of laughter and song as the conga line twisted and turned and danced and doubled back on itself. At the end of the song, everyone collapsed into giggles or sent up a rousing cheer. David Blakely was one of the first to break away from the line. Finding nobody serving at the bar, he went behind the counter to get himself a drink. A pair of hands rested gently on his hips.

'Are your eyelashes real?' asked Ruth, softly.

'Everybody says they'd look better on a girl.'

'I think they look very nice on you.'

He turned to face her and she touched his eyelashes gently. David was close enough to smell her perfume and he forgot all about the drink that he had been after. He had somehow known that this moment would arrive and he was ready to take full advantage of it.

'Hello,' he murmured with a sly smile.

'Hello . . .'

'Where do you live?'

She looked upwards. 'Over the shop.'

'Can I take you home tonight?'

Ruth needed only a second to make up her mind.

'Yes,' she said.

It was nearly 3 A.M. when they finally tottered upstairs to the flat. Ruth first made sure that her son was asleep and then led the way to her bedroom. She kicked off her shoes, unzipped her dress and stepped out of it, then lay on the bed in her underclothes. David tore off his jacket and dropped it to the floor as he clambered on to the bed after her. The first feverish kiss seemed to last forever and it left them both breathless. Ruth quickly undid his buttons and helped him off with his clothes. She pulled off his shoes without bothering to untie the laces. Aided by his eager fingers, she took off her underclothes and stockings then lay naked beneath him.

They kissed and writhed and passionately explored. As they broke from another long, searching kiss, Ruth laughed and cupped his chin in her hand.

'I don't know anything at all about you, Mr Blakely.'

'You soon will, Mrs Ellis,' he promised.

'How old are you?'

'Twenty-four.'

'I'm twenty-seven,' she teased.

'Don't worry. I prefer older women.'

His tongue was inside her mouth again and they rolled

against each other violently. Then she took him in her hands and guided him into her. It was over very quickly and they both lay exhausted and panting for several minutes. He ran a hand through her hair.

'I love you,' he whispered.

Ruth laughed quietly at him. 'Everybody does. Why should you be any different?'

'I want you to love me,' he said, seriously.

'Oh yes . . .'

'I wish you didn't work in this place!'

'You talk too much, Mr Blakely,' she decided.

Ruth rolled over so that she was on top of him. As she looked deep into his eyes, her gaze was at once affectionate and mocking. Earlier in the evening she had disliked him intensely and yet she was now lying in bed with him. She could still not understand how it had happened. David tried to speak but she put a finger on his lips. He moved it aside and lifted his head to kiss her very softly on the cheek. His face then clouded over with suspicion.

'Has Desmond ever slept in this bed with you?'

'No,' she replied, honestly. She mused on the matter and gave a wicked smile. 'Come to think of it, he must be the only man in London who hasn't.'

She burst out laughing and David did not know whether to believe her or not. Eventually, he joined in the laughter.

'Some people have got no shame!' he said.

'Some people have got enough for everybody.'

The laughter continued until well into the night. For Ruth Ellis, laughter – and life – would never be the same again.

2

Sunshine gilded the streets and brought out the shoppers in their hundreds. Traffic was thick, noisy and competitive and parking was a more severe problem than usual. It was a surprisingly mild day for early March and most people seemed to have discarded their heavy winter clothing and their thick fur-lined, crepe-soled boots. The two men unloading a van in the Brompton Road were actually working in shirtsleeves, humping crates of wine and spirits on to the pavement before carrying them up a flight of pink-carpeted stairs. The neon sign had now been switched off and the curtains on the club windows had been drawn right back. Daylight had robbed the Little Club of its allure and notoriety. It was the handbag shop that was doing the business. None of the passers-by gave the club a second glance.

'Is this the Little Club?'

There was one exception. The messenger from the florist shop was holding an ornate bouquet of long-stemmed red carnations that were wrapped in cellophane. He spoke to one of the men who was unloading the crates of alcohol from the van.

'It'd better be the Little Club, mate, or we've been lugging this booze up the wrong bleeding stairs.'

'I want Mrs Ellis,' said the messenger.

'Who doesn't!' chuckled the other. 'She's a cracker!'

'Where is she?'

'Up top.'

The messenger had to take his turn in the queue as the two men, each with a couple of crates, went slowly up the stairs. They turned in through the open door of the club itself and dumped their cargo beside the bar. Ruth Ellis, smart and businesslike in a dark green dress, checked the new stock then ticked it off on an invoice. The two men went off to fetch the next load.

'Mrs Ellis?' The messenger almost shouted. 'Mrs Ellis!'

Ruth could still not hear him. One of the cleaners was using a large hoover in the middle of the room and a portable radio was blaring out its music. The hubbub of traffic could be heard through the open windows and angry car horns were disputing a matter of access. Waving the flowers in front of her so that she saw the name written on the envelope, the messenger finally made contact with Ruth. She took the bouquet from him and the cellophane crackled. There was a small card inside the envelope. It was edged with a floral design and covered with spidery handwriting.

Dear Mrs Ellis,
When is your day off?
David Blakely.

Pleased and flattered, Ruth took the cellophane wrapping off the flowers and a dozen blooms spilled out on to the counter. She gathered them up and inhaled their scent for a few moments. Then she started to laugh very quietly to herself.

The cold weather had returned in earnest yet it had not deterred the crowds. They braved the wind and the damp in order to watch the afternoon's racing and their loyalty was rewarded with some spectacular driving and some equally spectacular accidents. Ruth Ellis had never been to a motor racing track before and this fact was obvious from her appearance. While everyone else was wearing duffle coats, sheepskins and warm boots, she had turned up in an excellent copy of a Chanel suit with a hat in matching colour. Fully-fashioned nylon stockings and high-heeled shoes completed the outfit. Among the hordes of racing fans, Ruth looked incongruous but quite stunning.

'Just look at her!' said Carole Findlater with scorn.

'She does rather stand out!' agreed her husband.

But Ruth was completely unselfconscious about her appearance. She had come to the track to enjoy herself and she did just that, cheering on the cars as they zoomed past, applauding the winners, and taking a keen interest in everything that was going on around her. When David himself was competing, she cheered even louder and urged him on whenever his car came within sight. After leaping up and down and waving her arms, she would wait breathless until the machines came around on another circuit.

'What ever does David *see* in her?' asked Carole.

'I would have thought that was obvious,' smiled her husband.

'She's a common tart!'

'She's his friend, Carole.'

'Well, she's not going to be mine.'

Carole Findlater was a short, slim, dark-haired woman in her early thirties. The thick, horn-rimmed spectacles gave her a rather studious air but this was offset by the vivid scarlet lipstick that she favoured. Her husband, Anthony, taller, quieter, more easy-going, was a couple of years older. He sported a moustache and a goatee beard. The Findlaters were close friends of David Blakely and they supported him whenever he was driving in a race. In fact, Anthony was David's mechanic. He was a true enthusiast and was captivated by the whole world of motor racing. His wife liked David too, but clearly not Ruth.

'Go on! Go on, David! You can do it!'

Ruth's voice was lost under the roar of the engines as the cars flashed down the strait once more. Driving with skill and audacity, David was staying in touch with the leaders. Ruth was thrilled by his performance and she cheered him until he vanished from sight around a bend.

Carole Findlater moved across to her.

'Wouldn't you see more if you wore your glasses, Ruth?'

'Men don't make passes at girls wearing glasses.'

'It would drive me mad.'

'What?'

'You must miss so much.'

'I'm vain,' giggled Ruth.

She turned to Carole in time to see a reproving look on her face. From the moment that David had introduced them, she had sensed the other woman's dislike of her, and had formed her own opinion if its cause.

'David tells me that you have two children.'

'That's right,' volunteered Ruth.

'A boy and a girl.'

'Andrea and Georgina. Andy lives with me.'

'And your daughter?'

'Oh, my sister looks after her.'

'I don't think I could bear to have someone else bringing up Francesca,' said Carole, righteously. 'I was brought up to believe that a mother should always take care of her own children.'

'I *do* take care of my own children,' defended Ruth.

'Look, I wasn't criticizing you,' soothed the other.

'It sounded like it to me . . .'

Anthony joined them and the tension eased at once.

'Enjoying it, Ruth?' he asked, pleasantly.

'Loving it!'

'Motor racing is magic. Nothing quite like it.'

'Is David going to win?' said Ruth, hopefully.

'He's doing his damnedest. If anything's going to let him down, it'll be the car. Just doesn't have the same power as some of the others. No, my money would be on

Cliff Davis. David will be there or thereabouts at the finish but I reckon Cliff has got it in the bag. Very few drivers to touch him in the 1500 c.c. class.'

'Someone's in trouble,' noted Carole.

'Where?' Her husband's curiosity was immediate.

Carole pointed towards a car that was limping into the pits with smoke billowing from under its bonnet. Mechanics came rushing to deal with the problem and to help the driver get out. Anthony identified the competitor at once.

'Poor old Geoff! Looks as if his engine's blown up on him. He's always unlucky, that man.' He headed for the pits. 'I'm going over to see exactly what the trouble is . . .'

The two women watched him hurrying towards the stricken car.

'Your husband's mad about racing, isn't he?' observed Ruth.

'David and Ant are two of a kind.'

'So I gathered.'

'David wants to spend his life driving cars and Ant just wants to tinker about with their engines. Be warned, Ruth.'

'What do you mean?'

'Men like that always put their cars first.' She shook her head ruefully. 'You finish up playing second fiddle.'

'Not me, Carole.'

'What's so special about you?'

Before Ruth could reply, the leading cars approached at high speed and she turned her attention back to the track. She began to yell encouragement to David then broke off as she saw that his car was behaving rather strangely. Pulling her glasses out of her handbag, she put them on so that she could have a better view.

'His car seems to be bouncing.'

'His liver needs a good shaking,' observed Carole, drily.

'What's wrong? Something in the engine?'

'Search me.'

'He's still going, that's the main thing.' She used her hands to form a megaphone. 'Well done, David! Keep it up!'

As the cars disappeared again, she slipped off her glasses and put them away again. Carole gave advice in a patronizing tone.

'Leave them on, Ruth. You obviously need them.'

'I don't miss much without them,' said Ruth, pointedly.

After three more laps, the race was over. A handful of cars were in contention down the final strait and only yards separated the first and second past the winning post. David was a comfortable fourth and he was elated that he had done so well in spite of the engine trouble that had plagued him towards the end. He was in his element as he rolled into the pits to receive the congratulations of his friends. Ruth soon arrived to give him a kiss and to tell him how impressed she was with his driving. David was delighted. He had been so anxious to show off in front of her and to fulfil all the boasts he had made about his car. But for his engine problems, he was convinced that he could have won the race. Ruth assured him that in her opinion he was the winner and she kissed him again.

They adjourned to the car park for a picnic with Carole and Anthony and they were soon joined by two other drivers, Cliff Davis and Clive Gunnell. Ruth had packed a hamper with food and champagne and the men applauded her when they saw the trouble that she had taken. The hamper was in the boot of David's grey-green Vanguard and they helped themselves beneath its raised lid.

With the exception of Carole Findlater, everyone seemed to be having a wonderful time, eating, drinking, joking, talking about the last race, making plans for the next one. Ruth now came into her own, acting as hostess, keeping everyone's glass topped up, laughing gaily at any horseplay. The car park was full of people enjoying similar picnics and she was conscious of all the eyes that she was managing to turn her way. David had had his moment out on the track: now it was her turn to blossom.

'We must have a snap taken!' insisted David.

'Lovely!' she agreed. 'All of us?'

'Just you and me.'

'Let me finish this first,' she said through a mouthful of chicken. 'Where's the camera?'.

Cliff Davis was elected as the photographer and he took his job seriously. David and Ruth stood beside the car he had driven in the race and waited while Cliff tried to focus the camera. Out of the corner of his eye, David noticed Carole glowering at them. He spoke to Ruth in an undertone.

'What do you think of Carole?'

'She's a stuck-up bitch!'

'But she's not,' he argued. 'She's fine when you get to know her.'

'Not sure that I want to, darling!'

'Watch the birdie!' called Cliff.

The couple smiled and the camera clicked.

'Let's have another for good measure!' decided David.

Cliff took the second photograph and then they went back to the picnic. They were soon laughing happily over another glass of champagne. Carole stood on the fringe of the group, pecking at a small apple and radiating disapproval. Clive Gunnell, helping himself to another leg of duck, noticed what she was eating.

'You can do better than that, Carole. Dig in.'

'No thanks,' she replied.

'But it's fantastic grub. Ruth's done us proud.'

'So I see . . .'

'Try some of this duck. It's delicious.'

'I'm not hungry.'

'Please yourself,' he said easily. 'But I'll tell you one

thing. There isn't a better picnic than this here today. Ruth is a real find. Very clever of David to bring her along.'

Carole forced a sweet smile and nodded. Anthony joined her.

'Everything all right, darling?'

'Yes!' she said, sarcastically. 'I'm having a whale of a time.'

'You might try and . . . mix in a bit more,' he suggested.

'With *her*? She's as common as muck.'

'That's not her fault.'

'No,' said Carole with condescension. 'It isn't. I suppose we ought to feel sorry for her.' Her jaw tightened. 'I certainly feel sorry for David. Does he realize what he's letting himself in for?'

At that moment David let out a peal of laughter at something that Ruth had said. He chatted animatedly with her for some minutes then he looked over her shoulder and produced his most charming smile.

Ruth swung round to see who was the object of such special attention from him. Several yards away was an attractive girl swathed in a shapeless Burberry and wearing high, sensible boots. She was grinning coyly at David and shifting from foot to foot. There was something rather gawky and immature about her but she had classical features and the unmistakable air of having been to an expensive girl's public school. Ruth disliked her on sight.

'Who's she?'

'An example of the sort of girl my mother wants me to marry.'

'Maybe you should show her an example of the sort of girl that *you* want to marry!' suggested Ruth.

David ignored her and went across to greet the girl with a kiss. Ruth felt a stab of envy as she watched them talking together. She took a vicious bite out of a sandwich and kept them under close surveillance. Cliff Davis sidled up to her.

'She's certainly one of the County set,' he commented.

'That's not what I'd call her!'

'Blakely fits in with that type,' he said, casually. 'Comes from a bit of a posh background himself. And there's no shortage of cash. They reckon that his stepfather is loaded.'

Ruth had seen enough and moved back towards the track. Cliff fell in beside her so that his shoulder was touching hers. The wind had got up now and it was causing people to button up their coats.

'Are you cold?' he asked.

'No. Is my nose red?'

'You'd be warmer sitting in the car.'

'I'm okay, thanks.'

They stopped within sight of the track. Another race was about to begin and the drivers were revving their engines impatiently as they waited for the starter's flag. Cliff made sure that nobody was within earshot before he spoke again.

'Are you really interested in all this?'

'Right now, I'm interested in another drink.'

'You do a fabulous picnic. I bet you were up all night rattling your pots and pans.' He put his face close to hers. 'You're a smashing girl, Ruth. I'd really like to get to know you better , d'you know that?'

'Yes!' she laughed. 'That's what they all say.'

'I mean it!'

'Don't let David see you flirting with me, Cliff.'

'What if he does? Will he hit me?'

'No, he'll hit me!'

They laughed together and then went back for more champagne.

* * *

Desmond Cussen sat in a restaurant over the remains of his lunch and toyed with the *Times* crossword. It had been a busy morning at the office and he had been glad to escape to the relative calm of the restaurant. Desmond was a director of the family business, a wholesale and retail tobacconist chain that had its head office nearby in Peckham High Street. He had come straight into the business after leaving the RAF and though the work was routinely dull, it gave him an appreciable income and a definite status. What the work did not do was to prevent him feeling lonely most of the time.

'Coffee, sir?' asked the waitress, coming up.

'Please. Black.'

She removed his plate and clacked away on her Cuban heels. Desmond pondered over a clue and tapped the end of his pen against his chin. An answer suggested itself and he quickly wrote the letters in the appropriate squares, only to realize immediately that he had made a mistake. He put a line through his answer and considered other possibilities. With a sigh of frustration, he rejected them all. When his coffee arrived, he abandoned the crossword altogether and simply read the paper. It was to be a profitable exercise.

He came to the listing of Forthcoming Marriages and ran his eye down the column. Something made him sit bolt upright in his chair. He took out his pen again and drew a circle around two names. Then he allowed himself a grim chuckle of satisfaction.

Morris Conley stood at the bar of the Little Club and played the Jolly Good Fellow. He fraternized with the customers, bought them an occasional drink, told dirty jokes galore. Dressed in a cream coat with a large green silk handkerchief cascading out of its top pocket, he looked sleek and prosperous. When he chatted to one of the club hostesses, his manner was jovial and avuncular.

The woman sitting at a table with Ruth noticed him at once.

'Who's that?'

'Morrie. He's the boss.'

'God, he's revolting!'

'There's plenty worse than Morrie, believe me.'

'Does he come in here a lot?'

'No, he usually lets me get on with running the place my way. Morrie's got other clubs besides this one and he also owns property in various parts of London. Also . . .' Ruth decided that she had said enough about her employer's business dealings. 'Put it this way, darling. Morrie's got a finger in a lot of pies.'

'He's still revolting!' decided her friend.

'Well, he's no oil painting, Sandra. I'll admit that.'

Ruth was glad that Sandra had called in to see her. They had been friends since childhood and although their lives had taken them in different directions, they had always managed to keep in touch. While Ruth had struggled on through setbacks and crises, Sandra had opted for a conventional marriage and four children. It was not proving to be enough. She had become disillusioned and restive and was haunted by the idea that she was missing out on something. And so she had visited her old friend.

A sudden influx of customers got Ruth to her feet.

'Time for me to go and do my stuff, darling.'

'I'll just sit here in the corner and watch.'

'Are you sure that you want to, Sandra? I mean, this is not exactly a Sunday School, you know. I'd hate it if . . .'

'Just forget about me, love,' assured the other. 'I'm a big girl now. I can take care of myself.'

Ruth squeezed her shoulder affectionately and walked off.

For the next couple of hours, Sandra was hypnotized. The club filled up and got rowdier in every way. Ruth presided over it all as if it was second nature to her, circulating freely, throwing off bright, brittle remarks, keeping everyone drinking, letting some of the men flirt outrageously with her, helping behind the bar when it became besieged. Though Sandra was shocked by some of the foul language that her friend was using, she found herself admiring Ruth's expertise at handling the customers and getting them to part with their money. The till behind the bar never stopped singing.

When it was all over and the guests had left, Sandra finally had a moment alone with Ruth, who flopped down in the chair beside her.

'Well, what's the verdict, Sandra?'

'You were right about it not being a Sunday School . . .'

'Oh, tonight was nothing!' Ruth told her. 'You should see us when things really liven up around here!'

'I still think that I could cope.'

'Cope?'

'As one of your hostesses.'

'You?' Ruth was taken aback. '*You*, Sandra!'

'Well, why not? My figure is not too bad even though I have had four kids. And I'm as pretty as you.'

'Thanks a lot!'

'I didn't mean it that way, Ruth.'

'You look smashing. Years younger than me.'

'So – when do I start?'

'You don't, Sandra. This is not for you.'

'But I've watched how it's done,' argued the other, 'and there's nothing to it. I can chat them up and get them to buy drinks and listen to their stories. Just like you.'

'There's a bit more to it than that, darling.'

'I don't mind the late hours, if that's what you're on about.'

'But you'd mind what goes with them . . .'

'Eh?'

Ruth spelled it out. 'Some of our hostesses are still on duty, Sandra. Upstairs. It happens. You get asked and it's not always a good idea to refuse.'

'Oh . . .' The colour had drained from Sandra's face.

'Then there's Morrie . . . Remember him?'

'He was disgusting!'

'Well, he's part of the deal.'

Sandra looked as if she was about to be sick. She realized how naive she had been and quickly lost all interest in the idea of working at the club. She stared in horror at her friend.

'You have? . . . With him?'

'We all have, darling.'

'Ruth, how *could* you?'

'It goes with the job,' she said, flatly. 'Still want it?'

David Blakely drove along a wooded road in Buckinghamshire on a fine Monday morning. He was returning to London after spending his usual weekend with his family at Penn. It had been a pleasant and restful couple of days. His mother, as always, had tended to cosset him. His stepfather, the wealthy Humphrey Cook, had talked cars with him for hours on end. And his nanny, who still looked after him with the same unthinking devotion that she had shown for so many years, made sure that he had everything he wanted without having to make any effort to get it. David had enjoyed the visit and yet he was very anxious to get back. London held something for him that was much more exciting than anything the village of Penn could offer.

As he rounded a bend at speed, the keys dangling from the ignition swung on their gold ring. He put a hand down to steady them and felt something that had only recently been put there. It was the best present that Ruth Ellis could have given him.

The key to her flat.

He pressed his foot down hard on the accelerator.

'London still leads in sports and country clothes. This warm red and green checkwool blouse ties with a bootlace bow at the neck and is worn with beautifully-cut grey worsted Daks . . . a chunky rib green collar from Curtis seen with their brown green worsted skirt . . . the skirt has centre sunray-stitched pleats at the back and two front pockets . . . the blond suede shoes with crêpe soles are made by Fenestrier of France . . .'

The female compère spoke smoothly into the microphone and described everything in great detail as the girls paraded around the small stage. It was a high-class fashion show and the people packed into the tea room at Harrods were being shown a wide range of clothing by experienced models.

Desmond Cussen glanced around and saw that he was virtually the only man in the room. It gave him an odd sense of importance. Ruth, beside him at the table, watched the show with utter fascination and made a note of any outfit that particularly appealed to her. She had already made several purchases at the store and the packages were stacked on a spare chair. Desmond wondered what had prompted her sudden interest in country clothing.

'Are you taking up golf?' he asked.

'Look at those ghastly shoes!' she said as a model strolled in to show them off. 'I wouldn't be seen dead in them!' When the next girl came in to display her outfit, however, Ruth was complimentary. 'Now that's the sort of look I want, Desmond. Such wonderful boots! I must have a pair of boots like that.'

'Has Blakely invited you to go racing again?'

'A lady never tells.'

'For his sake, is it? All this country clobber?'

'Can't you just see me in those boots, darling?'

'He's not worth it, Ruth.'

'What man ever is?'

'He's making a fool of you. Blakely's engaged to be married.'

There was a long pause as Ruth tried to absorb the impact of what she had just heard. She knew instinctively that Desmond had told her the truth. What hurt her most was the fact that she was not altogether surprised. It was as if she had seen something like this coming and pretended that it was not there.

'Recently?' she enquired.

'I saw it in the *Times* last week.'

Desmond pulled out his wallet and extracted the cutting that he had been saving for her. Ruth took it from him with a steady hand and read out the two names that had been ringed with blue ink.

'David Moffat Drummond Blakely . . . Mary Newton Dawson . . .'

'I . . . thought you ought to know . . .'

'And who is Miss Mary Newton Dawson when she's at home?'

Desmond shrugged. 'His fiancée . . .'

'He's incorrigible!' she said, dismissively. 'Well, I'll just have to go racing with you instead, Desmond. I've no intention of wasting all these clothes.' She put consoling fingers on his arm. 'Haven't you been bored to death all afternoon?'

'I enjoy shopping with you, Ruth.'

'Do have another sandwich,' she offered, passing the plate.

Another model was twirling gracefully in front of the audience. Ruth stared at her but saw nothing. The pain of betrayal was starting to bite much deeper. All that she could think about was revenge.

The taxi fought its way gallantly through the heavy traffic in the West End then pulled up outside a large florist shop. Ruth got out but left all her packages on the back seat. The driver lowered his window so that he could speak to her. It was Desmond Cussen. One of his favourite tricks was to dress up as a London cabbie and drive his friends around. Though the joke had worn thin for most of those friends, it still gave Desmond enormous fun. He played the part to the hilt and affected a Cockney accent.

'Shall I wait, Mum?'

'You can get pinched for impersonating a cabbie,' Ruth said, rather tartly.

'The meter doesn't work.'

'I prefer the Zephyr.'

Ruth marched off into the shop. Desmond looked at the palm of his hand as if he had just been given a handsome tip. His index finger touched the peak of his cap in gratitude.

'Gawd bless you, Mum . . .'

Inside the shop, Ruth went straight over to an assistant. She knew exactly what she wanted and her tone was peremptory.

'I want to send two dozen red carnations . . .'

'Of course, madam. When would you like them delivered?'

'Today.'

'If you could give me the name and address, please,' said the assistant, picking up a pen and a pad.

'Mr David Blakely, Assistant Catering Manager, The Hyde Park Hotel, Knightsbridge . . .'

'And the message?' asked the girl, scribbling quickly.

'Mr Blakely, congratulations on your forthcoming marriage. Please return front door key immediately.'

The girl looked up nervously at her then wrote down the message as dictated. Ruth then took the pen from her and wrote 'Mrs Ellis' with a flourish at the foot of the message.

Straightening her back, she smiled icily at the assistant. 'And how much will that be, dear?'

Ruth felt much better when she went out to the taxi.

David Blakely stood at the bar of the Steering Wheel Club and ordered yet another drink. He was in a somnolent mood and ignored most of the greetings and remarks that were directed at him. Completely out of key with the convivial atmosphere, he took his drink to a quiet corner and brooded in silence. It was only a matter of minutes before his glass was empty once more. He stared into it and saw a distorted reflection of his face. It looked pale and drawn and the dark eyes were enlarged grotesquely. He lowered his lids. Someone clapped him on the shoulder and jerked him out of his reverie.

'Hello, David, old boy! Congrats on the engagement!'

David swung round and glowered at the man before pushing rudely past him and heading for the bar. He stayed there until closing time.

A long night's work had left Ruth Ellis feeling very tired and she was asleep almost as soon as her head touched the pillow. Within an hour she was dragged out of her slumber by the noise of her bedroom door being flung open. As she sat up, shocked and frightened, a large bunch of red carnations was tossed unceremoniously on to the bed. When she realised that David Blakely was standing in the doorway, her fear gave way to white hot anger. He himself was clearly seething.

'You can keep your bloody flowers, Mrs Ellis!'

'My front door key!' she demanded. 'And don't shout! Andrea's asleep.'

They continued the argument in loud whispers.

'I don't want to be mixed up with a divorced night club hostess with two children!'

'If you don't like it, David Blakely, you can lump it!'

'I want you out of my hair – for good!'

'That suits me fine!'

'You'll miss me.'

'Oh, bugger off!'

'You will!' he boasted. 'You won't find another like me.'

'You're all the same!' she said with disgust, then held out her hand. 'Now give me the key.'

'I'm keeping it.'

'I'll call the police if you don't leave me alone.'

He swayed about unsteadily. 'You can call the Brigade of Guards for all I care!'

They glared venomously at each other in the half-dark and then they both burst out laughing. David lost his balance and fell on to the bed. The carnations were squashed beneath him.

'They cost a fortune,' said Ruth, reprovingly.

'Shall I put them in water?'

'Shush!'

She pulled him to her as he tried to rise and stroked his hair. They lay quietly together and let their anger ebb gently away. Ruth could smell the alcohol on his breath. She kissed him softly.

'And I'm not a divorced night club hostess,' she reminded him. 'I'm still married to George, legally, and I'm a manageress. I run that fucking place downstairs.'

'I prefer this fucking place up here,' he murmured.

'So do I.' She kissed him again. 'Who is she?'

'Mm?'

'The girl. Mary Bloody Whatsername?'

'Oh. Nobody . . .'

'And *are* you going to marry her?'

'Shouldn't think so.'

'Then why did you get engaged?'

'It . . . sort of happened,' he said, helplessly.

She bit him playfully on the cheek then started to help

him off with his clothes. His rage had gone now and it had been replaced by an almost childish need for reassurance.

'Who told you?' he asked.

'Desmond.'

'I didn't think you'd care.'

'You should have told me,' she scolded, gently.

'I thought you'd send me away if I did.'

Ruth smiled sadly. 'I fancy you too much . . .'

The red carnations were soon scattered all over the floor, crushed, forgotten and dying.

3

Carole Findlater was still working at her typewriter when Anthony got back to their flat in Tanza Road. He could hear her tapping away on the keys as he let himself in, went to the kitchen and made a pot of tea. After letting it stand for a while, he poured out two cups and took one of them through to Carole. Her face was a picture of concentration, brow furrowed, lips compressed, eyes puckered behind the horn-rimmed spectacles. It was only when she came to the end of a sentence and paused that she realized he was there.

Anthony put the tea down beside her on the desk.

'Oh, thanks . . .' She noticed the thumb-print on the saucer. 'You might have washed your hands first, Ant!'

'Sorry.' He wiped his fingers against his dungarees.

'If you must play about with that car all day long, the least you can do is to clean up before you come home.'

'Look, I'm sorry,' he soothed. 'Anyway, I don't "play about" with the car. I work damned hard on it.'

'For what, though? Ten pounds a week!'

'It's all David can afford to pay me.'

'And he doesn't always remember to give you that,' she added, warming to her theme. 'You should never have given up your job with Aston Martin.'

'Don't start all that again!' he sighed.

'But it's true, Ant. Our standard of living has gone right down since we moved to Hampstead. It was so different when we were at Colet Gardens. We used to eat out a lot. Go for a drink regularly . . .'

'That was when *you* had a full-time job, Carole.'

'I *had* to give up work when Francesca was born,' she

pointed out, reasonably. 'Let's face it, I had no choice. But you did. You packed in a steady job to get involved in this hare-brained scheme of David's.'

'It's not hare-brained!' he argued.

'You really think it will succeed?'

'Of course!'

'I wish I had your faith.'

'We know about cars, Carole. Just you wait. The Emperor will make us all rich one day.'

'One day!' she sneered.

'Now don't be like that . . .'

'Pigs might fly – one day!'

Anthony took a deep breath and made an effort to remain calm. Tolerant and undemanding by nature, he was all for a quiet life and hated rows or upset. He tried to pacify his wife by explaining it all to her once again.

'You can't expect to design and build a new sports car in five minutes. It's a slow process. You have to experiment, adjust, refine. But when the prototype is ready – and when it's proven itself in a race – then we'll be laughing. David reckons we could ask a thousand quid a time. Maybe twelve-fifty. If we get orders to build a whole fleet of them . . .'

'If . . .' she said, wearily. 'What about right *now*, Ant? How do we pay the bills and meet our commitments?'

'We'll manage somehow,' he assured her. 'Things will pick up now that you've started to write your articles again. We'll survive, Carole. We always have . . .'

'I want to do more than just survive,' she told him.

She sipped her tea disconsolately. Anthony could see that he had not convinced her and he searched for a way to cheer her up. He remembered what David Blakely had said to him earlier as they worked on Emperor. Without pausing to consider if it was altogether wise, he blurted out the invitation.

'Why don't we go out for a drink one night with David?'

'David . . .?'

'He suggested we make up a foursome. You, me, Ruth and him.'

Carole tensed instantly. 'And where are we supposed to have this drink? In that dreadful club of hers?'

'She could get an evening off. We'd go somewhere else.'

'No chance!'

'Why not?' He crouched down to reason with her. It won't harm us. Do us good to have a bit of fun.'

'Fun! With *that* woman!'

'David wants us to like her . . .'

'Well, he's wasting his time. I want nothing at all to do with Mrs Ruth Ellis. She's only one step up from a prostitute.'

'Carole! That's unfair . . .'

'It must cost a fortune to look as cheap as she does.'

'You want to see David again, don't you?' Carole was about to answer but decided against it. She moved away. 'It would only be for a couple of hours. We could stand her that long, couldn't we?'

'I couldn't stand her for a couple of minutes!' she said, spinning around on him. 'If David wants us to go out in a foursome, he can bring someone else. His sister. But I am not going to make any effort to be nice to that tart!'

Anthony scratched his head and gave up. He blamed himself for even suggesting it and showered her with apologies. Carole told him that she had to finish her article and went back to the desk as soon as he left the room. But she was unable to work at first. Ruth Ellis would not let her. The memory of their abrasive meeting at the motor racing track haunted her and she kept hearing Ruth's tinny laugh. She had to summon up her full concentration before she could continue. After reading what she had already written, Carole began to pound the typewriter keys with a real vengeance.

* * *

Taking the lift to the third floor, David Blakely stepped out on to a thick carpet and strolled along the corridor. He looked suave and elegant in his dark suit and had freshened his after-shave in the staff bathroom. When he found the door that he was looking for, he smoothed back his hair and straightened his tie before he knocked.

'Who is it?' asked a female voice inside the room.

He opened the door by way of reply and went in.

'Oh, hello . . .'

She was a handsome, middle-aged woman and she had gone to some lengths to make the best of her appearance. He caught the aroma of her perfume as soon as he walked towards her. She gave him a warm smile then indicated the bottle of champagne in the ice bucket. David proceeded to open the bottle.

'Where did you say your husband was?' he asked, casually.

'Away on business.'

'That's very convenient.'

'I decided that I needed a break,' she explained, 'so I've come up to London for a few days.'

The champagne cork popped and he filled two glasses.

'What do you plan to do while you're here?'

'See the sights . . .'

It was well over an hour before he returned to his duties.

The end of another evening at the Little Club found its manageress sitting at a table with Desmond Cussen. He was as quiet and undemonstrative as usual but he was now plainly besotted with her. While Ruth knew that she could never return his obsessive kind of love, she had become very fond of him and had started to rely on him in a number of small ways. Alone of the many men she knew, Desmond Cussen listened to her. He was genuinely interested.

'And what happened then?'

'I got pregnant,' she admitted with a wan smile. 'My own fault. Bound to happen sooner or later. Another kid was the last thing I wanted just then. Well, Andrea was still only a toddler.'

'An abortion?'

'He paid for it, of course, but that didn't make it any the easier to go through with. The things I've done for bloody men!' She heard what she was saying and sat up in her chair. 'Hey! Why am I telling you all this?'

'Who was the father?' he persisted.

'Nobody you know,' she said, bitterly, 'and nobody *I* ever want to know again.' Her heavy sigh was close to a groan of despair. 'Honestly, Desmond, I'd love to get out of this whole rotten world! I'd love to be able to bring Andrea up properly. In a real house. Far away from all this . . .'

'It could happen,' he opined.

'I'd grab at the chance with both hands . . .'

'I might hold you to that,' he whispered.

Commotion at the bar now diverted Ruth. She clicked her tongue when she saw that the cause of it was David Blakely. He was standing at the bar with Cliff Davis and Anthony Findlater. Having already had more than enough to drink, he was demanding more from Christine but the barmaid was handling him with polite firmness.

'One more, Christine!' he insisted.

'The bar is closed,' she said.

'Oh come on. I'm not just another customer.'

'The bar's closed.'

'I'll report you to the manageress,' he warned her, jokingly. 'I have a lot of influence there, you know.' When Christine ignored him, he grabbed a soda siphon from the bar top and aimed it at her in fun. 'Come on. A drinkie. Stand and deliver.'

A few other customers were standing nearby. One of

them, a young jockey in a hound's tooth jacket, tried to help the barmaid.

'Give over, squire,' he said to David. 'The lady told you it's home time.'

David pressed his thumb down and squirted soda all over the jockey. The latter lost his temper and threw himself at David but Cliff and Anthony got in the way. The shielded their friend from the attack.

'I'll kill him!' yelled the jockey.

'That's what I'm afraid of,' said Anthony.

'Let me get at the sod!' The jockey wrenched himself free and aimed a punch at David but it caught Cliff instead. 'Sorry mate. That was meant for him . . .'

At the first sign of the brawl, Ruth had come over to them.

'What's going on here?' she asked.

The jockey wiped his face with a handkerchief. 'Some of your customers are a bit short of manners, Ruth,' he said.

'And some are a bit short!' retaliated David.

The jockey's friends had to restrain him from throwing another punch. Ruth apologized to him, calmed him down, and dabbed at his coat with a clean tea towel that Christine passed to her. After one last hostile glare at David, the jockey pulled himself together and went out with his friends. David waited until he was some distance away before yelling a final jibe.

'Give my love to Snow White!'

Ruth grabbed his arm. 'Do you want me to lose my job!'

Blame Christine,' said David. 'I only wanted a drink.'

'Finish that,' invited Anthony, thrusting the remains of his own drink into his friend's hand. 'I must go . . .'

Anthony waved a token goodbye and slipped out. David gulped down some of his drink and then tottered dangerously. Ruth had to support him for a second.

'Sit down before you fall down!'

'Leave him to me,' offered Cliff.

He helped David towards an empty chair and lowered him into it. Ruth was left alone at the bar with Christine. She returned the tea towel and shook her head ruefully.

'Why do they do it, Christine?'

'They're like kids. Only worse.'

'If he thinks he's spending the night with me after that, he's got another think coming.'

'Oh sure . . .' Christine sounded sceptical.

'He can go and stick it in somewhere else,' muttered Ruth.

The music of the club's traditional Last Dance boomed out of the record-player. It was a comedy polka and the hostesses did their best to get some of the surviving customers out on to the dance floor. There was a lot of shouting and jigging and general hilarity. Keen to avoid being shanghaied into dancing, Desmond Cussen got up from his table and sauntered towards the exit. Ruth stood in his way and tried to persuade him to join in the fun.

'Come on, Des. Shake it round a bit before you go.'

'Not tonight, Ruth.'

'You're getting old!' she teased.

'Maybe . . . Are you busy tomorrow?'

'I'm going to see my sister.'

'Do you want a lift over there?' he suggested.

'Oh, I couldn't put you to all that trouble,' said Ruth, knowing full well that she was going to do just that.

'No trouble, I promise you.'

'Would you mind?'

'Not in the least. My pleasure. I'll ring . . .'

She gave him a token kiss on the cheek and saw him out. The barmaid had listened to the exchange. As she tidied all the things off the counter, she nodded after Desmond.

'He really fancies you.'

'Tell me something new, Christine.'

'None of the other girls turn him on. Only you, Ruth.'

'I'll tell you my secret some time . . .'

She got a tray and began to collect the empty glasses from the tables, taking care to give the dancers a wide berth. Cliff Davis was one of the few giving a passable imitation of the polka and she called out encouragement to him. He whooped back at her.

Ruth finally worked her way round to the table where David was sitting on his own, drunk, dishevelled and beaming stupidly.

'Hello,' he said, waving a few fingers.

She was scornful. 'Is your horrible appearance the result of having a good time?' she asked. 'Next time you roll up at my club in that state, you'll be turned away at the door.'

'You'd never turn me away,' he challenged.

'Try me.'

He went to sip his drink but she took the glass and put it on her tray. David groaned in protest then suddenly began to feel the effects of all the alcohol he had consumed. The room swam in front of him for a second and he had to put a hand to his head.

'Can I go upstairs.'

'For a minute,' Ruth said, involuntarily.

'Come with me . . .'

She helped him up. 'I won't be long . . .'

The music had now reached its height and the record had switched itself off automatically. Guests and hostesses made their way to the exit. David staggered off after them, using the tables and the wall to support him. Christine watched him until he had gone out of the door and curled her lip in disapproval.

Ruth brought the empty glasses back to the bar then came around it to take a look inside the till. A fat wad of notes was held down by a spring and there was plenty of silver as well.

'Looks nice,' she closed the till. 'I'll cash up in the morning.' She searched around under the bar. 'Have you seen my glasses anywhere?'

'Here,' said Christine, finding them at once.

Ruth sensed that her friend disapproved of David.

'Now don't get snotty with me, Christine,' she warned.

'I thought he wasn't staying the night?'

'He isn't.'

'Are you taking bets on that?'

'Look, it's my bloody flat!' Ruth relaxed at once and tried to shrug it off. 'You take him too seriously.'

'I don't take any of them seriously,' said Christine, coldly. 'They've still got their mother's milk dribbling down their chins.'

The barmaid put the dirty glasses in water to soak then found her coat and left. Ruth locked up and made her way upstairs. When she opened the door of the flat, David was facing her, sprawled out in a chair and still fully dressed. His eyes were closed. Ruth went to stand right over him. He peered at her from under his lids.

'I feel terrible . . .'

'That's nothing to how you look!'

'Why is it that you can drink all night and not get sloshed?'

'I'm a professional and you're just an amateur.' She gave his leg a kick. 'Now shift yourself. I want to sleep so you must go home to your mother.'

'I can go in the morning.'

'Go now!'

'Like this?'

'Maybe she ought to know the kind of son she's got . . .'

'I don't want to sleep without you,' he pleaded, softly.

Ruth sighed and resigned herself to his staying. She opened the convertible sofa-bed and turned back the sheets, then she crossed to her son's bedroom and opened the door as quietly as she could. She first slipped off her dress and hung it up in the wardrobe then she took out some pillows. Andrea began to talk in his sleep.

'They were looking for fish . . .'

Ruth sat on the bed and looked down at her nine-year old son.

'Did they find it?' she asked.

'I've got to take a packed lunch . . .'

He turned over and lay silent. She touched his head with the back of her hand then crept out of the room with the pillows. The bedroom door was shut carefully behind her.

David was already in bed, completely naked, his clothes an untidy heap on the floor. Ruth drew the heavy curtains to let in the light from the full moon and she opened the window a few inches. She then took off the rest of her clothes, put the pillows on the bed and got in beside David. Almost automatically, she wrapped her arms around him and he allowed himself to be embraced, resting his head on her shoulder. She stroked his hair.

'You've got to stop causing trouble downstairs,' she said, firmly. 'People don't like it and neither do I.'

'I'm a privileged customer.'

'I don't mind high spirits but yours have the habit of turning nasty. Now be warned.'

'Christ!' he exclaimed. 'Anybody'd think we were talking about the Ritz instead of a tatty little nightclub full of deadbeats.'

'You wouldn't be allowed a drink on credit at the Ritz,' she reminded him. 'That's another thing that's got to stop.'

He sulked for a moment then ran a finger up her arm.

'You spend too much time with Cussen.'

'He's a friend.'

'He's after you.'

'So what? Free country.'

'Not that he'd ever have the guts to do anything about

it!' sneered David. 'Except follow you round like a little dog.'

'Well, you know what they say about still waters.'

'His waters are not still. They're stagnant.' He giggled then he became serious. 'I wish you'd get out of this business, Ruth.'

'And do what?'

'You could marry me.'

'Ask me to do that when you've broken off your engagement to Miss Ponsonby Farnes Barnes from Yorkshire!' she retorted.

'Just leave her out of it.'

'You've got a nerve laying down the law about me flirting with other men! You've got the nerve of Old Nick!'

He waited a minute or so before he broke the news to her.

'I'm going to France on Tuesday.'

'Why?'

'Driving. Le Mans.'

'What's that?' She was baffled.

'Ask Andy.'

'Will you send us a card? He likes the stamps.'

David yawned. 'Go to sleep . . .'

'Bloody men!' she moaned.

'You should know.'

'Go to sleep.'

Within seconds they had both drifted into a deep sleep.

Ruth woke next morning to find the sunlight streaming in. Andrea was standing beside the bed, prodding her shoulder and staring nervously at the naked man who was in bed with his mother. Ruth opened a bleary eye and saw that her son was dressed for school.

'What is it, Andy?'

'I need my dinner money.'

She rolled out of bed and pulled on a silk nightgown. Then she found her handbag, fumbled inside, found some money and gave it to him. After smartening him up a little, she kissed him absent-mindedly on the forehead and walked downstairs with him. He opened the door and went out into the street without a word. Ruth picked up the milk and climbed the stairs.

When she got back to the flat, David was still fast asleep. She found that she had no urge at all to get back into bed with him.

The beach was relatively deserted and they were able to choose their spot. Andrea played with his bucket and spade near the water's edge, digging a large hole in the shingle so that it would be filled by the incoming tide. Gulls swooped and wheeled in the cloudless sky and added their cries to the gentle plash of the waves and the distant murmur of traffic. Out in the bay, a small boat was making its leisurely way towards the pier across the mottled surface of the sea. One lone swimmer had braved the cold water.

Ruth Ellis sat further up the beach with Desmond Cussen. She was wearing a sun-hat, a bright dress and sandals. Desmond, by contrast, wore dark trousers, a pale jacket over shirt and tie, and a pair of thick socks. His only concession to the holiday spirit was the hideous brown strap sandals. He held his face up to catch the breeze and inhaled deeply.

'It's so bracing here! I love the South Coast.'

'Me, too,' agreed Ruth. 'I was born in a seaside town.'

'You told me you came from Manchester . . .'

'Did I? Yes, well, that's only partly true.'

'I'm lost,' confessed Desmond.

'Quite simple, really. I sort of started off in Manchester because that's where I was conceived, but then Mum and Dad moved. My brother had this sleeping sickness, you see, and the doctor said that the sea air would do him good so the family moved to Rhyl. That's where I was born,' she announced with a sad smile. '74 West Parade.'

'I never knew that.'

'There's lots of things you don't know about me.'

'Yes . . .'

He glanced along the beach in time to see a wire-haired terrier trot up to one of the iron supports beneath the pier, sniff carefully, then cock its leg and leave its autograph. Desmond turned away to watch Andrea who was now experimenting with sandcastles, making a ring of them to act as a fortification against the sea. The boy was completely engrossed in what he was doing and Desmond drew his mother's attention to the fact.

'We'll have a job getting him off this beach,' she said.

'There's no hurry.'

'It's all so new to him.'

Desmond scratched at his moustache. 'Have you ever thought what's going to happen to him when he gets older?'

'I want him to go to boarding school.'

'It'd be the best thing if you go on working at the club.'

Ruth sighed. 'I can't see myself giving it up just yet.'

'Could you afford a boarding school?'

'Not at the moment,' she admitted.

'If you're strapped for cash, you know I'd always help . . .'

'I know you would.'

Having planted the idea, Desmond said no more on the subject.

Andrea was still burrowing in the shingle to get at the sand then scooping it out with his bucket and patting it firm with the back of his spade. He turned out yet another miniature sandcastle to guard the perimeter of the hole he had dug. The sea lapped right up to his heels and he scampered out of its reach.

'He's enjoying himself,' observed his mother.

'I wish you were.'

She looked at him for a moment then suddenly brightened.

'Come on, Des. Happy snaps!'

'What?'

'Well, you brought that fancy camera of yours, didn't you?'

Ruth got up and trotted across to a boat which was lying further along the beach. Desmond followed her with his camera. She struck a pose and gave him a broad smile.

'You're good at this,' he chuckled. 'I like it.'

'I picked it up in my Camera Club days,' she explained, adopting another pose for him and lifting the hem of her dress. 'But we had to show a bit more than a leg.'

'Keep still!' he urged, taking the photograph. 'Hold it!'

'They never had film in their cameras, you know. Have you? That's when I came to the conclusion that all men are stark, staring mad!' Her pose became even more provocative. 'How's this?'

'Perfect!'

Desmond was grinning happily, taking one snap after another.

Half an hour later, when Andrea had finally been prised away from his digging, they went into the Amusement Arcade on the pier. Desmond changed half a crown at a little glass booth and handed some of the pennies to Andrea. He vanished at once to spend them.

Ruth and Desmond wandered among the machines and had a go on the ones that appealed to them. She shrieked with laughter when she beat him at ice hockey but he got his revenge at football. It was pleasant, unforced, aimless fun. Then Ruth caught sight of a machine with a steering wheel on its front. Behind the glass panel, a tiny racing driver sat in his car, waiting to go on another twisting journey over a metal cylinder. David came into her mind. She quickly dismissed him and turned to another machine.

'Let's have a go at this one, Des.'

'You first . . .'

He put the penny into the slot and pushed it home. Ruth grasped the handle and squeezed hard. Beneath the bold challenge "How Sexy Are You?" was a list of possible answers. Ruth giggled when a light flashed on behind the word "Kissable".

'That goes with out saying,' he complimented.

'Now you have a turn.'

Before he could do so, however, Andrea came hurtling up to them.

'Any more pennies?'

'Here,' said Desmond, giving him half a dozen.

The boy shot off again and Desmond was able to take his turn on the machine. When he squeezed the handle, a light came up behind the word "Cuddlesome". Ruth nudged him and he smiled, shyly.

They meandered on to the Rifle Range. A series of clay pipes had been set up on racks and white balls were bouncing about on the top of water spouts. Desmond paid the man and was handed a rifle. He was a good shot and hit his target almost every time.

'Do you do this every Sunday afternoon?' she said, impressed.

'Just a knack,' he shrugged.

He paid for another go and looked down the barrel of the gun.

'Did you really mean it?' asked Ruth, casually.

'What?'

'About helping me to send Andy to school?'

'Yes.'

'I'll pay you back when I can.'

'Don't worry about that,' he said and shattered two clay pipes.

'You're a terrific shot!'

He kept firing. 'Would he mind going away from home?'

'Whenever I've mentioned it, he's always been keen on the idea.'

'We ought to be getting some information together about it,' he decided, turning to her. 'If we find a decent place, he could start next September.'

She nodded then took the rifle. 'Shall I have a go?'

Desmond stood behind her and showed her how to aim it. As he instructed her, he got closer and closer until he was nestled up against her. Ruth did not seem to mind.

With his mouth dry and his heart pounding, David Blakely stood in his little painted circle along with the other drivers. Facing them was a line of shining cars parked in echelon in front of the pits. The Le Mans 24-hour Grand Prix d'Endurance was by far the biggest and most important race that David had entered and he was determined to make his mark in it. He was hoping for a class win or a good placing in the Performance Index handicap to set the seal on his driving career. As the seconds ticked away to four o'clock, he ran his eyes over some of the other cars – Ferraris, Aston Martins, Jaguars, Mercedes. He would be up against the finest cars in the world and the best drivers. The élite had come to Le Mans. He was out to join it. Knees splayed and bent, he tensed himself for the signal to start.

When the flag dropped, a great roar of encouragement went up from the packed enclosures. The drivers sprinted across the track, leaped into their cars, started them up, then surged forward in a deafening thunder of exhausts, raising a huge cloud of dust as they sped away under the Dunlop bridge down to the Esses. David swerved and weaved and jockeyed for position. He was well towards the back but he had lost all trace of nerves now. With his adrenalin flowing and his competitive instinct heightened, he pushed his car to the limit and overtook three other machines.

Everything seemed to be happening much faster than during practice. The bends came at him quicker, the hazards confronted him with less warning, the constant nagging threat of other drivers on his tail forced him into split-second decisions. In no time at all, it seemed, he was screaming past the pits once more. His speed for the first lap was in excess of 100 m.p.h.

David was happy, excited and totally committed.

The small audience had scattered itself all round the cinema for the afternoon performance. Wearing her glasses, Ruth Ellis sat beside Andrea and watched Johnny Weissmuller bring another Tarzan adventure to its predictable conclusion. As the closing credits came up on the screen, long, transparent curtains swished across then opened almost immediately as the Gaumont British News began.

The first item was a film report on the crusade of Billy Graham. Surrounded by a battery of microphones, the tall, muscular, compelling figure addressed an enormous gathering, one hand holding an open Bible and the other bunched and lifted in the air. Without understanding a word of what was being said, Andrea sat in open-mouthed awe. There was a final shot of the evangelist holding both arms wide and looking up to heaven and then his glowing face disappeared.

Stirring background music now indicated a change of item and pace, the commentator's voice took on a brighter, more hectic tone.

'The cream of the motor racing world gathered in France last week to contest one of the most unique and exhilarating races in the calendar. Le Mans can always be guaranteed to give us plenty of thrills and spills and this year was no exception. For twenty-four punishing hours, the cars lapped the circuit at phenomenal speeds. The big question, of course, was – could Jaguar do it again? They won last year but could they hold off the might of the Continentals again . . .?'

Ruth's face was expressionless as she watched the drivers run to their cars and jump in. Andrea turned to look at her but she kept her eyes on the screen. An accident was shown in graphic detail.

A tall, thin, middle-aged man came into the auditorium, peered around in the gloom and saw Ruth. With dozens of empty seats to sit in, he chose instead to go into the empty row directly behind her. He sat down quietly and leaned forward so that his elbows were resting on the seat beside Ruth. She did not even turn around. As the second news item came to a close, she got up, took Andrea by the hand and led him out of the cinema.

Remaining patrons now saw film of the H-Bomb test at Eniwetok.

'"An interesting point was the presence of four generations of one family at the party, where otherwise there were very few grown-ups. They were: Caroline's lovely mother, Mrs Oliver Fitzherbert, her grandmother, Mrs Harold Hague, and her great grandmother, Mrs Tennyson Shafto . . ."'

'Try something else,' said Ruth.

She was sitting at the dressing table in her bedroom, putting on her make-up with great care. For close work, she used a gold powder compact which had a musical device fitted to it so that it played *La Vie En Rose* whenever she opened it. The compact was a treasured possession and she slipped it into her bag when she had finished with it. In the mirror, she could see Andrea leafing through a copy of the *Tatler* in search of something else to read out to her.

The boy cleared his throat. '"I was interested to hear that other young girls finishing at . . . at Les . . . Les . . .' I don't know this word,' he said, blankly.

'Show me.' She popped on her glasses.

'Right here,' he pointed.

'It's French. I think.' Her accent was atrocious but that did not deter her. '"Les Ambassadrices . . ."'

'What does it mean?'

Ruth studied the column to find out. 'It's the name of a finishing school in Switzerland . . .'

'What's a finishing school?' he wondered.

'It's a place where young ladies go to finish their education. They learn how to cook and sew and fill in divorce papers.'

'Did you go to one?'

'No.'

He put the magazine aside. 'Can I stop now?'

'Yes. You read very well.' She examined her completed make-up in the mirror and then turned around for his opinion. 'Gorgeous or gruesome?'

'Gruesome!' he said, dodging away.

'I've told you not to tell lies to your mother,' she warned, grabbing him playfully by the arm. 'I've got to go now.'

'Will he be there?'

'Who?' Andrea made no reply and an affectionate moment was suddenly cut short. 'Bedtime,' announced his mother.

They went through into the bedroom and he got into bed.

'He's making a racing car. It's called The Emperor.'

'How discreet!' she noted. 'Who's "he"?'

There was a pause. 'I want a pair of goggles. Real ones. Not toy ones. Can I? For Christmas?'

Ruth said nothing. She looked down at her son as he lay there with the bedclothes pulled up to his chest. The face on the pillow was serious and watchful but in no way resentful. They stared at each other for some time in silent acknowledgement of the problem whose name was David Blakely. Then, instead of giving him his usual good night kiss, Ruth turned on her heel and walked out, her long dress rustling as she went. The door closed firmly behind her.

Andrea gazed up at the ceiling and listened for the sound of his mother's departure. He got out of bed, went across to the window and held back the curtain. It was not long before Ruth appeared on the pavement below. She was greeted by a short, smart man in a dinner jacket and bow tie, and she twirled around to show off her evening dress. He smiled and escorted her to his car.

Desmond Cussen drove Ruth off into the night.

4

The Banqueting Hall of the Park Lane Hotel was a riot of colour and noise. It had been chosen as the venue for the Annual Dance of the British Motor Racing Drivers' Club. Everyone connected with the sport seemed to be there. Team managers, drivers, mechanics, race marshals, wives, mistresses, friends, relatives, pressmen, photographers and all the flamboyant characters who made up the motor racing scene were packed into the hall. Dance music was being played by a famous orchestra and stretched above their heads was a banner across the whole stage welcoming the guests. A small army of waiters and waitresses was kept busy and extra staff had been put on the bar. An air of celebration hung over the whole proceedings.

Dancing was well under way by the time that Ruth and Desmond arrived. A waiter conducted them to their table and they ordered drinks. They had to raise their voices to be heard above the excited chatter all around them. Ruth felt at home immediately. She smiled at everyone and basked in the admiring glances that she was getting from all sides. Desmond was his usual taciturn self but he was relishing his role as her escort and he knew that many envious comments were being exchanged at the tables around them. The drinks arrived and he tipped the waiter generously.

David Blakely was dancing with his mother, a poised, handsome woman in a superb and costly evening dress. Carole and Anthony Findlater were dancing not far from them and Cliff Davis was also there, enjoying the proximity of a shapely girl in a blue gown. David had spotted

Ruth the moment she came through the double doors but it took her some time before she recognized him on the crowded dance floor. She nudged Desmond and pointed out what she had seen.

'I thought he was still in France?'

'So did I,' she remarked, 'but there's always a difference between what David says and what he does.'

'Who's the woman? She looks old enough to be his mother.'

Ruth giggled. 'She probably *is* his mother.'

The quickstep ended and the musicians launched straight into a lively rumba. Most of the couples, David and his mother among them, stayed on the dance floor and began to swing their hips. Ruth could not wait to join in the fun.

'How's your rumba, Des?'

'As good as yours.'

'Prove it.'

They got up and he led her by the hand to the dance floor. David saw them coming and watched from a distance over his mother's shoulder. Ruth was dancing with her accustomed flair and Desmond was showing a good command of the steps as well. They worked their way to the middle of the floor. When Ruth collected a steely glare from Carole Findlater, she replied with a glittering smile.

Desmond pulled her closer to him.

'Have you ever stayed here?'

'No.'

'We ought to try it one weekend,' he suggested, 'to find out if it's as good as they say.'

'You're getting very bold, Desmond,' she said, pretending to be mildly shocked. 'Inviting me for a dirty weekend . . .'

'I'm sorry . . .'

Ruth laughed. 'I'm only teasing you. Don't be embarrassed. Honestly, you're so shy sometimes.'

'Is that another way of saying that I'm boring?'

'Of course not.'

'Are you sure?'

'Yes. You're very special to me?'

'Am I?' he said with surprise.

'I calm down when I'm with you.'

'You've always seemed calm enough to me, Ruth.'

'That's because I've never lost my temper with you.'

'No . . .'

'You're lucky. It's not a pretty sight. When I lost my temper with my soon to be ex-husband, we always ended up fighting.'

Desmond was alarmed. 'He *hit* you?'

'Oh yes! Bloody hard, too . . .' She smiled ruefully. 'Sometimes I was glad that he did belt me. I used to hear myself going on and on and I wished I could stop because the sound of my voice was driving me round the bend!'

'He asked for all he got!'

'Poor old George!' she sighed. 'He's as glad as I am that it's over but he's come out of it much worse than I have.'

'Do you still see him?'

'Not if I can help it. I hear that he's hitting the bottle worse than ever now. God knows why he's still employed as a dentist! He's better at knocking teeth out these days than putting them in.'

'How did you meet him?'

'At one of Morrie's clubs. Where I meet all my men . . .' She became brisk. 'When I'm with you, Desmond, all I do is to talk about myself. I tell you everything. You must get sick and tired of it.'

'But I don't, Ruth . . .'

'You should tell me to shut up.'

The dance came to an end and she clapped her hands. As the orchestra started to play a slow foxtrot, Ruth and Desmond went back to their drinks. David and his mother also left the dance floor and Ruth kept them under close observation as they returned to their table. They were met by David's stepfather, Humphrey Cook, a big, smiling, distinguished-looking man with a cigar in one hand. After holding a chair back for his wife to sit down, he chatted amiably with David. Ruth noted the easy intimacy between the two men and the way that David fitted so snugly into the picture of a rich, middle class family having a special night out together. She was piqued and envious. She felt that she was on the outside looking in at a world that she could not enter.

Her view was suddenly obscured by Cliff Davis.

'Glad you made it,' he grinned.

'Lovely to be here!' she responded.

'What are you drinking, Cliff?' asked Desmond.

But Cliff was whisked away by his partner to join in the dance. Ruth looked back at David and saw that he was heading towards her.

'Would you like to dance?' he requested.

She excused herself from Desmond and went back to the dance floor. At once pleased and annoyed with David, she moved slowly around with him and then felt a slight kick on her toe.

'You dance like an ape!'

'Sorry . . .'

'When did you get back?'

'Weeks ago.'

'You've managed to stay away from me this long,' she sneered. 'Why spoil it now?'

'I suppose I must miss you.'

'Your mother wouldn't like to hear you talking that way. I saw you dancing with her. Very touching. I can't wait to invite her over for one of my coffee mornings!' David laughed and she gave him a sharp dig in the ribs. 'I hate you.'

'No, you don't . . .'

'Why didn't you get in touch?'

'I sent a post-card from France.'

'Since you came back, I meant.'

'I've been . . . very busy . . .'

'Who with? Your lovely fiancée?

'Ruth . . .'

'Or one of your old flames?' A thought struck her. 'It wasn't *her*, was it?' she challenged, indicating Carole Findlater. 'I bet she fancies you like mad. I'm sure it's one of the reasons she can't stand me. Was it her?'

'Don't be silly!'

The danced in silence for a while then passed close by Carole and Anthony. Ruth watched the other woman beadily then shook her head.

'No. I take back what I said. She looks far too brainy to have had it off with you!'

'For Christ's sake, Ruth!' protested David. 'Careless talk costs lives!'

The Findlaters danced past again. Ruth beamed regally at them.

It was the only time that Ruth and David were alone together all evening. As soon as the dance was over, he brought her back to her table and walked away. Desmond commented on his brusque manner.

'Take no notice. He's jealous of you, that's all.'

'Of me, Ruth?'

'That post-card from France had a P.S. about you.'

'What did it say?'

'"Love to Desmond!!!" Three exclamation marks.'

'Oh, I see . . .'

He did not know whether to be flattered or disturbed. And he kept wondering she had not mentioned it to him before.

Dancing and jollity continued until well past midnight then the guests began to drift away. Determined to end the occasion on a high note, Ruth ordered champagne and invited some of the stragglers across to her table to share it. David had been dancing with Carole and they were included in the invitation but they held back on the fringe of the group. The waiter brought the champagne and opened it with professional skill.

Cliff Davis accepted his glass with alacrity.

'What are we celebrating?'

'My divorce!' said Ruth.

David slipped away with Carole and went back to their table.

Desmond, Cliff and the others toasted Ruth and they drank the champagne. A great burst of raucous laughter was heard from the far side of the room where some drunken young men were having a battle with soda siphons and ice cubes. Ruth's voice suddenly sounded old and jaded.

'It's time those children were in bed. They're getting over-tired.' Music started once more. 'The Last Waltz . . .'

The main lighting now dimmed and the dancers moved around in a softer, more mysterious glow. Everybody seemed to be getting to their feet to join in. Desmond leaned over to Ruth.

'Has your divorce really come through?'

'Just wishful thinking.'

Her eyes were fixed on David's table. With the Findlaters, his mother and his stepfather, he formed a contented little group. The lights had dimmed right down now and the tables were virtually in darkness. Ruth could just make out David's outline as he led his mother to the dance floor for the final waltz. A spotlight was now playing on the couples and there was a dreamlike atmosphere. Ruth and Desmond were the only people not dancing.

They went quietly out of the room.

The Little Club had closed and its neon sign had been switched off. The premises were harmless and anonymous once more. A car drew up in the darkness and the driver got out and came around to open the passenger door. He escorted a woman across the pavement and waited while she fumbled for her key. As soon as she opened the door, his hopes of being invited in were shattered.

'Good night, Desmond. And thanks . . .'

'Good night . . .'

He had been given a peck on the cheek. He got back in his car and pondered. Those three exclamation marks had raised his expectations too high. And too soon. He drove slowly away.

Ruth, meanwhile, got to the top of the long climb and let herself into the flat. A surprise awaited her. The convertible sofa had been opened. Lying on it was David Blakely. Ruth stood in the doorway and let out a cry of amazement.

'Well, bounce my brains! Look who's here! What the hell do you think you're doing? Get out!'

'Good babysitters are hard to find,' he said lazily, 'and I'm one of the best.'

'I suppose you picked up the technique from your nanny.'

'That's right . . .'

'Maybe your nanny ought to work for me!'

'She's still got her hands full looking after me,' he said, reaching for a glass beside the bed. 'You look ravishing, by the way.'

'I see you helped yourself to the scotch.'

'That villainous employer of yours won't mind. All part of his generous entertainments allowance, isn't it?'

'It still has to be paid for. We're neither of us working to support the idle aristocracy.'

'You exaggerate my social standing.'

'I don't give a fiddler's fuck about your social standing! You've no business letting yourself in here when I'm not in!' She grabbed his coat and flung it at him. 'On your way!'

He shrugged. 'Well, at least Andy was pleased to see him.'

'Did you wake Andy?' she chided.

Ruth went quickly to her son's bedroom and inched the door open. She ignored David when he came up behind her and sneaked a quick kiss on her bare shoulders. Satisfied that Andrea was sound asleep again, she closed the door and turned to confront David.

'I'm going to teach him to drive as soon as he's old enough.'

'You won't be around that long,' she assured him.

He tried to kiss her again but she pushed him away. When she walked across the room, he went with her, staying very close and keeping in step with her. She smacked him off again.

'Don't play the fool!'

'I don't like being without you, Ruth,' he said, coaxing her to the bed. 'I need you at night.'

'Go and say that to your fiancée!' she retorted.

'I haven't got one any more. I broke it off.'

'You callous swine!'

'Bloody hell! Can't I do anything right?' A note of pleading intruded. 'I love you, Ruth.'

'You've got a funny way of showing it.'

'It's never happened before,' he said, simply.

'What are you going to do about it?' She took his glass and poured some whisky into it. 'Well?'

'I'm flat broke,' he admitted.

'Have you squandered your inheritance already?'

'It was only seven thousand quid.'

'*Only*! That would last me a lifetime.'

'I have a lot of expenses . . .'

'Yes! Chasing after women and getting engaged and showing off at the Steering Wheel Club – "Come on, chaps! I'm buying!" Money runs through your hands like water, David.' She sipped her drink. 'Isn't there *any* of it left?'

'What there was has gone on the Emperor. Building a sports car is an expensive game. I have to pay Ant a tenner a week. Then there's the rent for the warehouse. It's a constant drain.'

'Can't your tycoon stepfather bail you out?'

'I'm afraid not.'

'But he's mad about cars, isn't he?'

'Oh, he's interested in The Emperor. Wants progress reports and all that. But he won't put any cash into it.'

'I don't blame him.'

'He's never let me down before,' complained David, sulking.

'He hasn't let you down. He's a businessman. Before he puts money into anything as big as this, he wants to make sure it's serious.'

David looked helpless. 'I don't know what to do.'

'Andy's more capable of taking care of himself than you are . . .'

He accepted the reproach with a soulful nod. Ruth topped up the glass and went to sit beside him. She let him have the first drink and then sipped some more whisky herself. Her tone was at once sympathetic and practical.

'You lost that French race, didn't you?'

'You know damned well we did.'

'Do you really think you're a good driver, David?'

'You've seen me race,' he argued.

'I've never seen you win.'

He was deflated. 'You think I could chuck it in?'

He lay back with his head propped up on the pillows. Ruth remained sitting on the edge of the bed. Without touching each other, they seemed to get closer and a tranquil tenderness grew up between them. Ruth chose her words carefully.

'I don't mean give it up altogether. Just keep it as a hobby.'

'I only know about cars, Ruth. The Emperor isn't just

going to be a race-winner. It's the prototype of a specialist car that will sell for upwards of a thousand.'

'Are you panicking?' she asked.

'Yes.'

'I know the feeling.'

'I want to come and live here with you.'

'Don't be silly,' she scolded, gently. 'You can't run away from home just because your family's trying to make you stand on your own feet for once. Prove to your stepfather that you're serious and capable of sticking at one thing and he'll start coughing up again. You can't live here, anyway,' she added, glancing around. 'Morrie wouldn't like it. He'd start charging me rent.'

'Couldn't you go back to tarting for him?'

'Don't call me a tart.'

'I hate everything you did and everyone you knew before you met me!' he said with sudden anger.

'Take two aspirins and tell me about it in the morning,' she suggested with irony. 'I'm going to bed. I've got a business to run.'

She stood up and began to get undressed. David watched her remove her evening dress with care and put it on a clothes hanger which she then hooked over the curtain rail. She slipped off her shoes and then lifted the hem of her slip to undo her suspenders.

'I want to marry you, Ruth.'

'Why? Are you pregnant?'

'I won't have any peace until we're married.'

She stared hard at him. 'I've never had any peace . . .'

He let her remove her stockings and suspender belt and then he came over and embraced her. She was stiff and unresponsive as he tried to kiss and stroke her. He was pleading again now.

'I think about you all the time. We've got to be together.'

‘It’s not fair,’ she whispered.

‘I don’t want to quarrel with you.’

She slapped him across the face with both hands again and again. He held her wrists and got her under control then he backed towards the door of the flat which she had left open when she first entered. Sticking his leg out behind him, he kicked it shut.

With Ruth at once resisting and complying, he eased her back towards the bed. As they fell on it together, she gave a little cry of defeat and then kissed him hungrily. David took her straight away. He fell asleep while he was still on top of her and she had to roll from under him. As she lay there in the dark and listened to his stertorous breathing, her confusion and anguish returned.

Ruth hated him and yet she had let him stay. She loved him and yet she saw his treacheries and his weaknesses. He hurt her and yet she came back time and again for him to hurt her some more. She wondered what it was in her that made her behave the way she did. And she whispered aloud something she had said to David earlier.

‘I’ve never had any peace. Never . . .’

Desmond Cussen parked his car in Devonshire Street and walked up to his flat in Goodwood Court. It was a big, airy, well-furnished flat in a private block and he had decorated it to a bachelor’s taste. He opened a window, poured himself a drink, then took it through to his study along with his briefcase. He sat in front of his oak roll-top desk, allowed himself a drink, opened his briefcase and pulled out a parcel. He unwrapped it carefully to reveal a large, new, leather-bound photograph album. He opened it at the first blank page. Then he took out a small folder of snaps from one of the drawers.

After a second drink, he went straight to work. Within a quarter of an hour, it was all over. Ruth Ellis was staring up at him in a dozen snaps taken at a beach on the South Coast. She was smiling and posing and teasing him with her body.

Desmond grinned. In the photographs, she was his.

The manager sent for him as soon as he arrived that morning. David knew what to expect but he affected surprise all the same. It was not in his nature to let anyone talk down to him.

'You're late, Mr Blakely.' The manager was a small, fussy, well-groomed man of middle years. 'Not for the first time.'

'What do you mean?' asked David, bridling.

'I mean that your timekeeping is not good enough. You seem to think you can arrive late and leave early whenever you like.'

'That's not true!'

'Oh yes, it is. You treat this hotel as if you're a guest here, not an employee.' He peered over his rimless spectacles. 'You *work* here, Mr Blakely. We pay you.'

'Five measly pounds a week!'

'You accepted the terms of employment.'

'I'm worth more,' argued David.

'That's immaterial now.' The manager removed his spectacles and cleaned them with his handkerchief. 'Well, there's nothing more to be said, is there?'

'I don't follow . . .'

'We've put up with enough. You're dismissed.'

'You can't sack me!'

'I can and I have. Let's be realistic. You've never committed yourself to this job and you're always taking time off to go motor racing. Wherever your future lies, it's not in hotel management. I'm sure that you'll be glad to leave us.'

'Now hold on a minute!' said David, hotly. 'You can't just kick me out like this. My stepfather got me this job.

He has influence with your Board. He won't *let* you get rid of me.'

'That's a matter you'll have to take up with him.'

David changed tack. 'Please. Give me one more chance . . .'

'I'm sorry, Mr Blakely. I can't.'

'You don't know how awkward this could be for me!'

'That's your concern. Goodbye . . .'

'All right!' sneered the other. 'Keep your job!'

The manager replaced his spectacles and crossed to the door to open it wide. David strode out with battered pride. He went to the tiny office to collect his things, feeling both annoyed and relieved. There would be an embarrassing scene to face with his stepfather but he was now free of a job that he had always despised. He tried to convince himself that it was all for the best. From now on he would be able to devote himself full-time to motor racing and achieve a real standing in the sport.

Minutes later, he walked out of hotel catering for good.

Carole Findlater put the suitcase on the bed and opened it. She began to pack it with the things that she would need for the trip. Shortage of money had forced her to take on more journalistic assignments but there was the occasional bonus. A magazine had now commissioned a series of articles from her about the lot of women in the Soviet Union. She was flying to Moscow for a few days and found the prospect quite exciting. It would mean leaving the baby in the care of the au pair girl and she was sure that the latter, with Anthony's help, would be able to cope. The visit to Russia had a number of attractions. It would be interesting, profitable and a form of escape. It would also be a status symbol.

She opened a drawer and searched in it for a cardigan. Unable to find it there, she tried the drawer beneath it. Carole froze when she saw what was in front of her. It was a beautiful christening robe and it awoke some bitter memories. Weeks earlier, she and her husband had been at a party to celebrate David's birthday. Inevitably Ruth Ellis was there. A few acrid remarks had passed between the two women. Later in the evening, when Ruth had been indulging in some horseplay, she had squirted Carole with a soda siphon.

A fierce row had followed. Both Carole and Anthony had turned on David. They had told him exactly what they thought of his friend from the Little Club and they did not mince their words. Deeply upset by their reaction, David had been anxious to find some way to heal the breach and he had ordered Ruth to apologise to Carole. When Ruth had refused, he threatened to walk out on her. Reluctantly, and after much protest, Ruth had agreed to try to make it up with Carole. By way of an apology, she had bought Francesca a christening robe.

As Carole now looked down at it, she could hear Ruth's voice.

'It's a good one. It cost thirty guineas.'

Carole slammed the drawer shut. She was resolved about one thing. However expensive the christening robe had been, her daughter would never wear it.

A powerful sports car raced through the Buckinghamshire countryside and made light of any hills it had to go up. David Blakely was driving with a skill that had his passenger laughing in admiration. Excited by the great rush of air as they sped along, Ruth was happier than she had been for some time. She began to think that there was a future for David in motor racing and she wanted to be at his side to share his triumphs. As the car crested another rise and then plunged at breakneck speed down a long gradient, she understood why the sport was so exhilarating.

They eventually reached the village of Penn and David

slowed the car down as he approached. A fine old half-timbered pub stood on the edge of the village and David parked a short distance from it. He got out of the car and she tried to follow him.

'Just wait here a minute,' he insisted.

'Why?'

'I want to make sure my mother isn't there.'

'Wouldn't her car be parked here if she was inside?' she asked.

'Sometimes they walk to the pub,' he explained.

Ruth was rebellious. 'If you think I'm sitting out here while you warm your arse in the Inglenook, you've got another think coming!'

'You said you wouldn't make a fuss if I brought you here!'

'I want a drink . . .'

'If you're going to meet my mother,' he reasoned, 'I've got to break it to her gently.'

She was suddenly calm and resigned. He came round to her side of the car as she opened her handbag and took out a bottle of scent. She dabbed some of the scent behind her ears and looked up at him. David spread his hands in a gesture of apology.

'It's all right,' she said. 'I understand.'

'It's nothing against you, Ruth.'

'As long as you're not ashamed of me . . .'

'Don't be ridiculous!'

He bent down to give her a token kiss and she splashed some of her scent on his cheek. She giggled at his expression.

'Now we both smell the same.'

'I won't be long,' he promised.

'You'd better not be. Now run along. I'll talk to myself while you're gone.'

David strolled across to the pub and went into the lounge bar. Ruth got out of the car and looked down the road towards the village itself. It was at its best in the early afternoon sun, picturesque, peaceful and redolent of a wealthy and leisured world. She walked a little way down the road until she came to a beautiful Tudor cottage standing in half an acre of well-established garden.

Ruth gazed at it with undisguised envy. She reflected that her whole life had been one long succession of moves and changes and sudden upheavals. She had never been allowed to settle anywhere. It was time to put an end to all that. She owed it to herself and to her children to find a better life and a proper home. She decided that it was time to put down roots.

She went back to the car and reclined against the bonnet. Because David had not returned, she assumed that his mother must be inside the pub and tried to imagine what he was saying to her. It had taken a lot of persuasion to get David to bring her out to Penn. Ruth knew that it was an important step forward in their relationship.

It was not long before the door of the pub opened. Out came a group of middle-aged people in walking attire. Chatting together, they went past Ruth without even noticing her and headed up the road in a solid body of tweed and cashmere. In the middle of the group, she thought she glimpsed David's mother, striding along purposefully in thick brogues with the aid of a walking stick.

David now emerged from the pub with a drink in his hand. He crossed over to her and handed it to her. Without a word, she got into the car and began to sip the gin and tonic.

'Okay?' he asked.

'What did your mother say?'

'I didn't really get a chance to speak to her, I'm afraid. The Rambling Club were there in force.' He saw her purse her lips in annoyance. 'Ruth, I *will* talk to her, I promise. But it's not the kind of thing that can be rushed.'

'How long have you been saying that?'

'You don't know my mother,' he said.

'And I'm not likely to at this rate!'

'Just give me time!' After a moment's hesitation, he got into the driving seat and started up the engine. 'Would you like to see the house or are you still angry with me?'

'Take me to see the house.'

David turned the car round and drove off in the opposite direction to that taken by the walking party. The vehicle soon slowed down and turned left into a narrow leafy lane. Ruth was able to reach out a hand and touch the hedge with the tips of her fingers. They eventually came to a gateway and David swung the nose of the car in through it. Ruth caught her first sight of the house.

It was enormous. She had expected it to be large but the sheer size and grandeur of the property took her breath away. It was a stately Georgian building in fine decorative order and it was set in a huge, landscaped garden that also contained tennis courts and a swimming pool.

David stopped the car outside the house.

'Do you want to come inside?'

'No,' she said. 'Your mother'd have forty fits if she found out I'd been in her home.'

'Do you want to walk around the garden?'

'No.'

'My stepfather fell for this place. Likes to play the Lord of the Manor. One of the Old School. You'd be amazed at some of the things he does.' He laughed, shortly. 'Do you know, he still has a cobbler call at the house regularly to see what shoes need to be mended. And he even has a clockmaker in to wind all the clocks for him. Talk about living in the past!' He turned to Ruth. 'What do you think?'

'I was expecting something more on the lines of the Palace of Versailles,' she said, sipping her drink. 'Did your mother like the way you smelled?'

'You asked me to bring you here.'

'I'm glad you did. There's no future in this for me. Take me back to London.'

'Give it time . . .' he urged.

'Just drive, David.'

He put the car in gear and drove violently away from the house.

5

It was early evening at the Little Club and business was slack. The hostesses chatted together over drinks, the barmaid checked the float in the till, and the receptionist sat in a corner with a newspaper. Seated at the piano, the club's newest employee was playing a soulful version of *I Still Believe* but nobody was really listening. The tedium of waiting had given the place a bored, listless air.

Ruth Ellis was standing at the bar with Desmond Cussen, almost the only customer to have arrived. She stubbed out a cigarette and took another from the silver case that he instantly produced from his pocket. As he lighted her cigarette with his Ronson, she nodded across at the pianist.

'What do you think of her?'

'I've heard worse.'

'She gives the place a bit of class.'

'I suppose so . . .'

'Also, she's good, ornamental value. Especially in that dress. The customers love to lean on the piano and get a grandstand view of those tits.'

'She can play well,' he conceded.

Ruth inhaled on her cigarette. 'My father was a musician. The cello. I think he was really talented. Used to play in this trio that went round the cinemas. Of course, there was a demand for it in those days when they still had silent films.' She grimaced. 'Then along came the Talkies and Dad was out of a job. That's when our problems really started. Must have been awful for him. To have a talent that nobody wanted any more. He never got over it . . .'

'Are you musical yourself?' he asked.

'My instrument is the record-player!' she giggled.

The telephone on the bar rang and Christine answered it.

'Hello? . . .' She smiled when she heard who it was. 'Andrea wants you upstairs, Ruth.'

'Calling long-distance was he? Come on, Des.'

She led Desmond out through the door and up the stairs. They let themselves into the flat but there was no sign of the boy.

'We're here!' called Ruth.

Andrea came marching out of his bedroom in his new school uniform. The dark blazer and cap had matching badges on them and the tie had diagonal stripes. White knees poked out from beneath the short grey trousers and the grey socks had reached different altitudes on the chunky legs. He was obviously very proud of the uniform and desperate for Desmond's approval.

'You look very smart,' said Desmond.

'All my clothes have got my name on them. Look . . .'

He took Desmond across to a large trunk with its lid open.

It was packed with clothes and books and all the other required paraphernalia for a pupil at boarding school. Andrea turned over a vest and showed the name-tape sewn into it. Tucked in the corner of the trunk was a dog-eared collection of child's toys. Ruth decided to check the contents and got down on her knees. Her son immediately went on the defensive.

'I need everything . . .'

'We'll see . . .'

She began to rummage through the trunk and brought up odd items for inspection. Desmond watched them until he became aware that someone was standing behind him. He swung round. Lounging in the open doorway was David Blakely. Unshaven and unkempt, he was in crumpled old clothes and his hands were filthy with grease. He had obviously been working on The Emperor. Judging by his expression, it had not been very productive work. He was sour, moody, resentful.

Ruth looked up to be met by an accusatory stare. Desmond noted the flash of fear in her eyes. It was Andrea who broke the silence.

'This is my new school uniform.'

'Is it?' said David without interest.

'And my trunk.'

'Yes . . . I need a drink.'

'The Club is open,' advised Desmond.

But David had already lurched across the room to the cocktail cabinet. He opened it and helped himself to a glass of neat gin.

'Anyone else?' he asked.

Ruth did not know what to do or say. Anxious to avoid any kind of row with David, she decided that escape was her best course of action. She got up from the trunk and made for the door.

'I must get back,' she said on the move. 'Make sure he puts everything away properly, won't you, Desmond?'

The two men were suddenly left alone with the boy. David threw down his drink and then mustered a faint curiosity in Andrea.

'When do you go?'

'On Monday.'

'Looking forward to it?'

'Yes.'

'Why?'

The boy shrugged. David went over to the trunk and pulled a ragged gollywog out of it. He gave a mocking laugh.

'You can't take this,' he said. 'They'll tear the legs off. And yours.'

'Did they do that when you went to school?' asked Andrea.

'Yes.'

'He's teasing you, Andy,' reassured Desmond.

David tossed the golliwog back into the trunk and glanced idly through the rest of the contents. Then he turned back to Andy and scrutinized the uniform more carefully. He noticed something clipped into the boy's top pocket.

'New pen?'

'Yes.' Andrea took out the fountain pen for inspection and unscrewed the top. 'It's a gold nib.'

'Good. A present?'

'From Uncle Desmond.'

'Very generous of you – "Uncle Desmond".'

'Take your uniform off and hang it up, Andy,' said Desmond.

The boy obediently gathered up his things and went off into his bedroom to change. Desmond went across to the cocktail cabinet and poured himself a drink. David crossed over to him and held out his now empty glass.

'I could do with a refill.' He watched as Desmond tipped some gin into his glass. 'Come on. Be generous. Morrie's paying.'

'Mr Conley is not a philanthropist,' noted Desmond.

'Did you know he'd been inside?'

'It doesn't surprise me. What for?'

'Fraud, I think. Or living off immoral earnings. Ask Ruth.'

There was an awkward pause. Desmond gulped down some whisky.

'Still working on The Emperor?'

'That's all I ever do now. Everybody seems to think I'm flogging a dead horse.'

'Findlater's a first class mechanic .

'Ant has been a brick. Don't know what I'd do without him.'

While the men were trying to manufacture a conversation that neither of them was enjoying, Christine came into the flat through the still open door with two of the club hostesses. The women were anxious to pet and pamper Andrea for one last time before he left. They went straight into his bedroom to see his uniform and their voices cooed and trilled in admiration.

Desmond watched them come in then turned back to David.

'What state is the car in?'

'We've still got a long way to go,' sighed David.

'When do you think she'll be ready to race?'

'I don't know. In the Spring, maybe.'

'It'll be worth it when you win.'

'*If* I win . . .'

'You've got to make yourself win,' urged Desmond with an uncharacteristic laugh. 'I found that out when I was flying during the war. You need to go beyond the limit to find out what you're made of.' David was staring at him in surprise. 'I used to tell myself I don't care if I die, just so long as I go in really hard this time . . .'

'I'll . . . bear that in mind,' said David.

Andrea came out of the bedroom. 'Can I come and watch you win, David?' he asked.

Desmond spoke curtly. 'No Andy. You'll be at school.'

The boy shrugged and went back to the three women.

It was almost midnight by the time that Anthony Findlater returned to Tanza Road. He had expected his wife either to have gone to bed or to be waiting up vengefully to tax him with his staying out late yet again. When he let himself into the flat, however, he was given a pleasant surprise. Carole was still up but there was no hint of reproach in her manner. She was curled up on the sofa reading a novel and seemed to be in a very contented mood. He soon learned why.

'They rang me this afternoon and they're going to commission another series of articles.'

'Well done, darling!'

'It'll keep the wolf from the door for a bit longer.'

'It's great news! We ought to celebrate.'

'We will,' she reminded him. 'At your birthday party.'

'Yes, that . . .'

'Don't tell me you'd forgotten, Ant?'

'No, no, of course not.' His face crinkled into an apology. 'Sorry I'm late. Can't seem to leave that damn car alone.'

'I'll make you a cocoa,' she offered.

He followed her through into the kitchen and they compared their days. Anthony was startled to realize that he had worked on The Emperor for over fourteen hours. Carole was clearly delighted with her latest success and her husband took advantage of her good mood to tell her something that he had hesitated to mention before.

'Everything ready for the party on Saturday?'

'More or less . . .'

'I invited David.'

'Good.'

'He wants to bring Ruth.'

Carole's manner changed in a flash. 'No,' she announced.

'I don't like her any more than you do but – '

'No, Ant. That woman is not coming into my home.'

'David *asked*. As a special favour.'

'Favour!'

She was almost shaking with rage and he elected to back off. They took their cocoa through to the living room. He steered her on to safer topics and her anger gradually abated. By the time that they went to bed, some of her good humour had returned.

As they lay in the darkness, he whispered to her.

'I told David he could bring her.'

'What?'

'It's *my* birthday, Carole . . .'

He dropped asleep long before she did.

It was fun to go back. Since he had been dismissed from the Hyde Park Hotel, David Blakely had derived great pleasure from going there with his friends and behaving obnoxiously in public. It was a form of revenge. As he sat with Ruth Ellis at a table in the main bar, he talked far too loud and brayed at anything that was remotely funny. It was late morning. Ruth, as usual, was paying for the drinks.

'Have you tackled your stepfather yet?'

'He won't give me a penny,' moaned David. 'Says that he wants to see results first. What bloody results? We need the money in order to *get* any results.'

'Keep your voice down. Everyone's looking.'

'Let them . . .'

Ruth sighed. 'Well, at least you got some cash out of your real father. That's more than I ever did.'

'Yes, he was a smashing chap, my father. You'd have liked him.'

'If I'd been allowed to meet him,' she observed, tartly.

'I was only a child when they got divorced . . .'

'Why did they split up?'

'I told you. Another woman.'

'But you've never given me the gory details.'

'I don't want to,' he said evasively.

'Afraid I might be shocked?' she teased.

'Let's have another drink . . .'

'Tell me what happened first. I'd really like to know.'

David became almost shy. 'Another time, maybe.'

'What are you hiding?'

'Nothing!' he said, defensively.

'Nothing!' she echoed, mimicking him. They giggled together then she became serious. 'Tell me. Please, David.'

He thought for a moment then dropped his voice. 'Okay. I will. But I don't want you spreading it around, Ruth.'

'You can trust me, darling. I know how to keep a secret.'

He breathed in through his nose a few times and then he began.

'She was a patient of his. The other woman.'

'And?'

'She died.'

'What of?'

'I can't remember the medical term for it. The point is that they blamed my father.' He moved close so that his head was almost touching hers. 'They put him on trial. For murder.'

'Murder?' Ruth was aghast.

'Yes. They claimed that he'd had it off with the girl and that when she got pregnant, he'd given her drugs to induce an abortion. That was how she died, you see.'

'Poor girl!'

'She was an out-of-work waitress, apparently. Phyllis something.'

'Go on,' encouraged Ruth, spellbound.

'My father admitted that he'd had an affair but pleaded that if that was a crime then most of Sheffield ought to be on trial.'

'And most of London!' she added. 'Oh sorry. I didn't mean to interrupt . . . What about the drugs he was supposed to have given her?'

'He did prescribe something – he admitted that. But he swore on oath that it couldn't have done her any harm.' The defensive note crept in again. 'My father was a respected doctor. He had a good reputation in Sheffield.'

'And was he the father of the child?' pressed Ruth.

'Who knows? The girl had several men. It could have been any one of them.' He emptied his glass. 'The case was dismissed.'

'I think I can guess the rest. His wife divorced him . . .'

David nodded. 'Mother couldn't forgive him. It was because the girl was only a waitress. Because she was common.'

'No wonder I haven't been introduced to mother.'

'Let's go,' he said, abruptly.

He took her by the hand and led her quickly out.

He stayed at the Steering Wheel Club until it was nearly closing time and then went on to his favourite haunt. As soon as he walked in, he knew that something was wrong. After looking all round the room, he went to the bar and hissed for Christine to come over. He was kept waiting while she served some customers but she eventually answered his summons. He did not need to say anything. The expression on his face was question enough. Christine was brisk.

'She's taken the night off, Mr Cussen.'

'Oh . . .'

'Gone to a party in Hampstead.'

He was wounded. 'She never told *me* . . .'

Desmond drove home to the solace of his flat.

Someone had brought a long-playing record by Ted Heath and His Band. A space had been cleared in the middle of the living room and most of the partygoers were dancing to the rhythm of the *ABC Mambo*. Ruth was by far the most skilful and sensuous dancer, setting an example to the others and inciting the men to lewd cheers by hitching up the hem of her dress in a provocative way. Almost as soon as she arrived at Tanza Road, she had the party revolving around her.

Predictably, it did not endear her to Carole Findlater.

She watched Ruth for as long as she could bear and then slipped away to Francesca's bedroom. When David found her, she was rocking the baby in her arms in the half-dark.

'Can't the au pair look after her, Carole?'

'I'd rather do it myself. I don't want to watch that little blonde bombshell of yours throwing herself at every man in the room.'

'She's enjoying herself,' said David, tolerantly.

'Good. I'm glad. That's what parties are for.'

He was saddened by the malice in her voice. Crouching beside her, he put an arm around her shoulder. Carole relaxed slightly.

'She's harmless, really,' he argued.

'She's dangerous, David!'

'You don't know Ruth . . .'

'If you were as obsessed with finishing that damned car as you are with her, The Emperor wouldn't still be a figment of your imagination!'

'You knew it wasn't going to be easy!' he whined.

'As usual, Ant's following your lead,' she complained. 'If you let him fiddle about with that thing for the rest of his life, he will. You've got to push him. He thinks that God will provide. If I don't.'

'Or me.'

'You already owe him three weeks' wages and he hasn't said anything, has he?'

'I don't need reminding, Carole.'

'Then don't talk as if he's some kind of sponger.'

At that moment, Anthony himself wandered into the room.

'What's up?' he asked.

'Carol's nagging me for bringing Ruth and for owing you money.'

'Well, I'm with her on both counts.'

'You let Ruth come, Ant,' needled his wife.

'I didn't think she'd be this bad.'

'She's always this bad!' snorted Carole.

'That's unfair!' said David, vehemently. He looked from one to the other of them then shrugged. 'I think she'd like me to marry her . . .'

Carole hooted derisively.

The record had now finished in the other room and everyone converged on the table that bore the drinks and the remnants of a cold buffet. Ruth let someone pour her a glass of wine and then she lifted it to Carole as the latter entered from the bedroom.

'It's a lovely party, Carole!'

'Glad you could come!' replied the other through clenched teeth.

Ruth raised her glass again. 'Happy Birthday, Anthony!'

Everyone took it up. 'Happy Birthday, Ant!'

Cliff Davis led the inevitable chorus.

David did not join in. He found himself watching Ruth with a mixture of fascination and distaste. For the first time, he was beginning to regret that he had brought her. He felt an impulse to get back at her, to punish her daring to spoil his friend's party.

Cliff Davis turned waiter. Grabbing a plate of canapés, he whisked them round the partygoers and then offered them to Carole.

'Not for me, thanks.'

'You haven't touched a thing all evening!' he protested. 'Not even mine!' He chuckled at his own joke then hailed Anthony. 'How long has your wife been off her food, Ant?'

'She eats like a bird,' said her husband.

Ruth seized on this. 'My son told me that birds eat twice their own weight every day.'

'Did they teach him that at his new school?' asked David.

'Yes.'

'It must be such a relief not to have him under your feet any more,' observed Carole, waspishly.

'Oh, he loves it,' said Ruth. 'It's worth every penny.'

David aimed the next remark right at her. 'She's only sorry that Desmond can't afford to send him to Eton.'

Ruth was suddenly on fire.

Music started up again and the dancing resumed. Though she joined in, she had lost all her zest and enjoyment. She drank glass after glass of the cheap red wine and for once it began to get to her. It made the fire inside her burn even more fiercely.

'Good night, everybody!'

'Good night!'

'Thanks for coming!'

'Cheerio!'

'We can see ourselves out!'

'Take care!'

'Don't do anything I wouldn't do!'

'Drive safely!'

They left in a flurry of farewells and came out into the cold drizzle of an autumn night. Ruth could barely contain her rage as they came down the stone steps and out on to the pavement. When they reached the car, she turned on him with sudden ferocity, eyes blazing and her whole body vibrating with anger, frustration and shame.

The words came hissing out of her like steam from a boiler.

'You despicable little shit! Did you bring me to this cut-price binge in the back of beyond to be humiliated by your friends? How dare you mention Andy's school fees! It's no business of theirs! You're so fucking disloyal! Betraying me in front of that po-faced cow.

David hit her viciously across the face.

She made no sound and neither did he. Both were shocked. He grabbed her, opened the passenger door, and bundled her in as if she were a naughty child who was in disgrace. Slamming the door behind her, he got into the car himself and switched on the ignition. He drove wildly, recklessly and obsessively all the way back.

Ruth sat there in fear as her face swelled and throbbed.

The piano was being tuned at the Little Club. Morris Conley looked at the instrument with utter disgust and wished that he had never sanctioned its purchase. He was not in the mood for music of any kind.

'Can't you tune that thing *quietly*!' he demanded.

'Sorry, sir,' mumbled the piano-tuner.

Conley sat down at the table again and regarded Ruth. It was only a few days since the party at Tanza Road and the bruising still showed on her face. Conley had no sympathy to offer.

'I don't like being taken advantage of, Ruth,' he warned. 'Your mind is not on your business and your business is to look after my business.' She made no answer. He continued more forcefully. 'Fair's fair. I prosper, you prosper. In that order! I let you live here free because you work for me, but I'm not providing board and lodging for that nickle-plated ponce who's moved in here with you. Unless you kick him out, I'll start charging you rent!'

Ruth recovered her voice. 'I'm not one of your girls, Morrie,' she said with defiance.

'Oh, yes you are!' he reminded her.

The pain in her face started up all over again.

The only consolation she had was the fact that she had seen it coming but her warnings had gone unheeded and her advice ignored. Carole stood in the Magdala pub with her husband and vented her fury. She had finally shaken off her sympathy with David.

'Honestly, he's so spineless!'

'Carole . . .'

'He's got no guts. No guts at all.'

'Look, he's going through a bad patch at the moment . . .'

'For God's sake, don't ask me to feel sorry for him, Ant. He's brought it upon himself and you know it.'

He nodded in agreement. 'Bit insulting to us, really.'

'Insulting!' The word seemed miserably inadequate to her.

The thing she feared most had now happened. David Blakely was living with and off Ruth Ellis. He was becoming more and more dependent on her and she was exploiting that dependence to get back at the Findlaters. She had given David an ultimatum. Unless he stopped visiting his friends in Tanza Road, he would no longer be welcome at the Little Club or at the flat above its premises. Ruth was driving a wedge between David and the Findlaters.

'After all we've done for him . . .' she protested.

'Don't let it upset you, Carole.'

'I mean, who does the woman think she is? What right does she have to push him around like that?'

Anthony sighed. 'Can't we just forget it for a while?

Carole did not even hear him. 'I've lost a lot of respect for David over this. I thought he had more fight in him. Yet he lets that creature dictate to him. It's shameful!'

'He'll come out of it in time.'

'Well, he needn't expect us to be there when he does.'

'But he's our friend,' said Anthony. 'Nothing changes that.'

In her heart, Carole knew that her husband was right. David was their special friend. He was the godfather of their child. It was cruel to surrender him to the clutches of Ruth Ellis. They should take positive steps to help him.

They would fight back.

* * *

The pianist had now established herself as an important feature of the Little Club. She would play requests for the customers until all hours and her repertoire seemed to be without limit. Ruth loved to hear her play *Would You Dance With a Stranger* because it was a song that had a special meaning for the manageress. Late one Saturday evening, when she heard the familiar chords again, she stood beside the piano with a large glass of Pernod in her hand and sang the words of the song. It was not a big performance. Ruth was singing more for her own benefit than anyone else's but most of the customers were listening to the sad, wistful voice.

'Would you dance with a stranger
On a night made for love?
Would you dance with a stranger
'Neath the stars up above . . .?'

It was the night before Remembrance Sunday and the Club was full with ex-servicemen, many of them in evening dress with their medals and ribbons attached. Desmond Cussen sat at a table with a group of ex-RAF friends, two of whom wore mess blues. Almost everyone in the room but Desmond was wearing a scarlet silk poppy and a tray of them stood on the counter next to a collecting box.

As Ruth's voice rose above the murmur all around her, Desmond watched with interest and concern. She seemed to have drunk far too much Pernod and a maudlin note had intruded. During her song, David Blakely escorted a poised and attractive young woman into the Club. Both were impeccably dressed and seemed to complement each other. David ordered drinks then listened to the songstress.

'Would you dance with a stranger
If that stranger were me . . .?'

Polite clapping followed but not everyone appreciated her voice. Excusing herself from the American veteran with whom she was sitting, Maryanne, one of the club hostesses, made for the Ladies' Toilet. She found a colleague, Barbara, there and pronounced her verdict on Ruth's performance.

'She sounds like a cockatoo with a cleft palate!'

'She's not too bad,' said Barbara, freshening her lipstick.

Maryanne peered into the mirror and started to repair her own make-up. She was a tall, slim, hard-faced girl with the sneering manner of the natural malcontent.

'I wish she'd give me the sack,' she observed, applying mascara. 'I'd like to have a sense of grievance.'

'You were born with a sense of grievance!' Barbara closed her full lips on a tissue paper then examined the result by pouting at herself in the mirror. 'Anyway, she's the one who'll get the sack if she doesn't watch out.'

'Serves her right!'

'She's making a real fool of herself over Lover Boy. Did you see him walk in just now? Who's his piece tonight?'

'Not his sister!' cackled Maryanne. 'But if anyone's a fool, it's old Droopy Drawers.'

'You mean Desmond?'

'Can't he see that she's stringing him along?'

'I'd like someone to adore me that much,' opined Barbara.

'I'd despise them!'

'You despise everyone.'

Maryanne turned to her. 'Your Yank isn't throwing much money around tonight.'

'He's broke.'

'Don't talk daft, Barbara. There's no such thing as a penniless Yank.' She adjusted the neckline of her dress. 'Oh well, I suppose we'd better get our busy little tits back in the bull ring!'

They laughed coarsely and went out together.

The pianist ended her stint with a few wartime

favourites that had the ex-servicemen floating on nostalgia. When she finally left the piano to warm applause, the record-player took over again. Ruth ordered another large glass of Pernod and sipped it with an edge of desperation. More guests arrived and she snapped into her routine welcome, insisting that they bought poppies from the tray and giving each one of them a kiss as she fixed the poppies in their lapels. David was standing further along the bar and she was studiously ignoring him. He hid his anger beneath a surface indifference and chatted easily to his partner. But he kept an eye on Ruth.

Desmond now came up to the bar and she saw that he had no poppy. He willingly parted with five shillings into the collecting box and she inserted the poppy in his buttonhole.

Christine was having less success with another customer.

'Come on, Wilf. Remembrance Day. Cough up.'

'I was a conscientious objector!' chortled the other.

There was general laughter and Ruth joined in. David took his partner by the hand and led her off into the room. Glad that they had gone, Ruth turned back to the bar and found that her empty glass had been refilled automatically by Christine.

One of Desmond's RAF friends now lurched up to them and tried to look down the front of Ruth's dress. He grinned drunkenly.

'I see you're not wearing your campaign medals, Mrs Ellis.'

'We weren't decorated for the kind of war work I did.'

'Munitions?'

'Service Corps.'

Boozy guffaws greeted the joke but they were short-lived. David came storming across the room with a record in his hand. He was clearly spoiling for a fight as he confronted Ruth.

'Have you seen the state this record's in!' he demanded.

'What?' She was baffled.

'This record I gave you! Look at it! Scratched to hell!'

'It's worn out because I play it all the time.'

'I suppose every bloody customer in the place has been handling it!' he yelled, waving the record in her face.

Ruth's control vanished. Resentment that had been building for a long time now spilled over in a torrent of fury.

'Oh, for God's sake!' she shrieked at him. 'Did you want me to put it in a safe deposit box at the bank! It's the only bloody thing you ever have given me. Stop behaving like a spoilt brat!'

David grabbed her drink from the bar and threw it over her. There was general commotion. Ruth swore, Christine screamed in surprise, and David's partner let out a moan of horror. Desmond leapt at David and grabbed him by the lapels.

'You stupid little swine!' hissed Desmond.

David fought back and a vicious brawl was brewing. Morris Conley appeared out of nowhere to take charge. Silence fell as he came bustling purposefully up. He pointed at David.

'You! Out!'

Taking him expertly by the throat, he guided him to the exit and ejected him with force. Red-faced and trembling, the young woman who had come in so happily with David now sneaked out after him. The incident had caused embarrassment all round and some of the customers decided that it was time to drink up and leave. Desmond made a gesture of apology towards Conley.

'Sorry . . .'

'Don't worry, Mr Cussens. All over now.' He smiled at the barmaid. 'Give the gentleman a drink, Christine.' The smile faded as he turned to Ruth. 'I want a word with you. Now.'

Ruth followed him meekly to a quiet corner of the room.

An hour later they had all gone. Ruth was left alone. Weary, dejected and humiliated, she put the money from the till into some cash bags, switched off the lights and let herself out. She had to drag herself up the stairs to the flat.

He was waiting for her at the top, swaying about and reeking of alcohol. When he opened his mouth to speak, she got in first.

'Do me a favour. Don't say you're sorry.'

'It's the bloody booze,' he explained.

'Stop drinking.'

'And you! It must be something in you, Ruth. All the men you get your claws into end up like this. The Mad Dentist didn't turn violent until he married you!' He goaded her. 'You must like it or something!'

'I love it, I love it, I love it!' she yelled, advancing up the stairs. 'Because of you, I've lost my bloody job!'

She grabbed his arm to push him out of the way.

'I'm going to sleep,' he burbled.

'Not in my bed!'

'Why not?'

'Get out and don't come back!'

'Ruth – '

'GET OUT!'

There was a brief scuffle and then he threw her backwards down the stairs. The cash bags fell with her and coins were scattered everywhere. He glowered at her without sympathy.

'You always say that – all of you – and whether you mean it or not, I always stay.'

He used his key to open the door to the flat then pulled it tight after him. Ruth lay there for several minutes before she got up. Instead of following him, she went back downstairs and unlocked the door to the Club. Putting on her glasses, she gazed around the place and felt her animosity surge. The Little Club held too many sour memories for her. It was a symbol of everything she had come to hate. She stood in front of the bar and surveyed it with calm disgust. Then slowly and systematically, she began to smash all the bottles and break all the glasses. Nothing in the Club was spared. She overturned tables and chairs, tore out electrical fixtures, savaged the curtains. Even the piano fell victim to her vengeance.

Only when the whole place had been comprehensively wrecked did she pause for breath. She looked around with deep satisfaction then she slipped off her glasses and put them in her bag.

Ruth Ellis went out into the street and walked away.

6

Desmond Cussen ignored the sharp pinch of a November wind and unloaded the last of the luggage from the boot of his Zephyr. After closing and locking the lid, he addressed himself to the problem of carrying everything at once. Standing on the pavement like a silent challenge to his strength and ingenuity, was an assortment of suitcases, carrier bags and parcels. Draped across them were some fashionable dresses and a few winter coats.

He met the challenge with alacrity and somehow managed to pick everything up at the first attempt. The clothes were thrown over his shoulder, the parcels were tucked under his arm, and his hands were free to cope with what remained.

'Well done, Des!' congratulated Ruth.

'Easy when you know how!'

She herself was loaded to capacity as well. Amongst other things, she was carrying some more coats, an elegant ladies' umbrella, and a brand new portable radio. Desmond nodded towards the block of flats and they set off.

'Can you manage?' she asked.

'I'm fine . . .'

When they reached the entrance to Goodwood Court, he indicated that she should go in first and she acknowledged this courtesy with a smile. They entered the building and began to ascend the stairs very slowly. Footsteps could be heard above and then an elderly, grey-haired man in a tweed suit appeared. Feeling obliged to say something, Desmond voted for a cheerful greeting.

'Morning, Arthur!'

'Oh. Good morning . . .'

The man nodded to Ruth and she bestowed a gracious smile on him.

They struggled on up the stairs until they came to Desmond's flat. He had left the lock on the catch so that they could push their way straight in. They dumped their luggage on the floor with a joint sigh of relief.

'Made it!' he said.

'Home sweet home . . .'

'Welcome to Goodwood Court!'

A thought chilled her. 'I'm glad it's not Goodwood Motor Racing Circuit!'

The lounge bar of The Crown public house was steadily filling up as Saturday evening wore on. It meant that David Blakely was never short of an admiring audience whom he could thrill with anecdotes about the motor racing world. Questions came from all directions.

'Have you ever met Fangio?'

'What's Stirling Moss like?'

'When will The Emperor be ready?'

'Is Mike Hawthorn really as good as they say?'

David accepted another drink and chose the question that he wanted to answer. The locals wanted to be impressed and he did not disappoint them.

'Mike Hawthorn and I are great pals . . .' It was not true but there was nobody to contradict him. 'He was telling me about a spot of bother he once had in the Ulster Trophy Race at Dundrod. Mike was driving Archie Bryde's Cooper-Bristol and he ran into serious trouble during practice . . .'

'What happened?' asked someone.

'Over-heating. The water pump packed in completely. There was no time to get a spare from England and so they had to ask around Belfast. Luckily, there was this retired major who owned a standard Bristol touring car which had the same type of water pump. He agreed to lend it to them.'

'The Army to the rescue again!'

'They worked all night but when they drove to the circuit next morning, they discovered another problem. The cylinder-head gasket was blowing into the water jacket pushing the water through the overflow pipe. Mike thought that was it. There was no way he'd be able to race . . .'

'Did he pull out?'

'No,' said David, basking in their rapt attention. 'Someone came up with the bright idea of putting mustard into the radiator to stop the leak.'

'Mustard!' The girl at his elbow was amazed.

'You're pulling our leg,' challenged a lone sceptic.

'It's true,' promised David. 'It really does do the trick sometimes. So they charged around the local cottages trying to beg, borrow and steal as many tins of Colman's mustard as they could. They shoved it all in the radiator and – hey presto! – it worked. The leak was cured and Mike was able to race.'

Everyone laughed appreciatively. Except the lone sceptic.

'And I suppose Hawthorn went on to win the race?'

David spoke airily. 'No, he finished second behind Taruffi in Tony Vandervell's Thin Wall Special.' He finished his drink and remembered another second-hand story. 'Taruffi! Now I could tell you something about *him* . . .'

'Ready for another drink, David?'

'Oh, thanks very much . . .'

'Tell us about Taruffi . . .'

David's regular visits to Penn were not made solely in order that he could see his mother and stepfather. They lifted his morale. Back in London he was a penniless playboy, struggling to make his name in the motor racing world: in the lounge bar at The Crown he was a famous driver who rubbed shoulders with the mightiest in the sport and who would soon launch his own race-winning car. The failures of London could be painted as successes in Penn. He always left the village with a boost to his ego.

Holding court in a local pub was not the only way he achieved that boost. When he had plundered his repertoire of tales about Mike Hawthorn and Taruffi and the other big names in the sport, he left The Crown and drove to a house on the other side of the village. There was a light in the front bedroom.

David, as usual, was expected.

She was a tall, impassive, well-groomed, well-preserved woman in her late forties and everything about her suggested that she had been a top model in her day. In a large dance studio with mirrors along the walls, she was trying to pass on her expertise to her students in the Beginner's Class. She put them through some basic exercizes in deportment and winced inwardly at the results. None of the students showed any special grace or aptitude. The platinum blonde in the red leotard was one of the better pupil-models but she was having trouble concentrating. The Principal dismissed the class and left the room with a sense of escape.

A man was lurking selfçonsciously in the corridor outside.

'She won't be long now, Mr Cussen,' said the Principal.

'Oh. Good. How is she getting on?'

'Early days yet. Too soon to say.'

'She's very keen.'

'Yes, that's an asset,' she agreed, neutrally. 'But you must excuse me. I have an interview to conduct . . .'

'Of course . . .'

She gave him a benign smile and sailed off down the corridor. Desmond paced up and down until the students began to emerge from the studio. He noted how much younger than Ruth the majority of them were. When she finally emerged, she was wearing casual clothes and a grin of achievement.

'How was it?' he wondered.

'You'll see me in *Vogue* next!'

'I can't wait.'

She tucked her arm through his and they sauntered down the corridor towards the exit. He had enrolled her for a course at the Model School because she had been so enthusiastic to join. Desmond was hoping that it would turn out to be a wise investment.

'I'll never be able to thank you for all you've done,' she said, squeezing his arm tight.

'My pleasure.'

'You're killing me with kindness . . .'

They left the building and walked around the corner. Instead of the Zephyr, he had brought the London cab and he fell into his usual role as the cabbie. He held the door open for her to get into the back seat then closed it behind her. He soon set the car in motion. When he had driven only a few hundred yards, he heard a tapping sound in his ear. Ruth was sitting on the jump seat and drumming her long red fingernails on the glass partition that separated driver and passenger. Desmond reached over and slid the partition back. She put a finger inside his shirt collar and ran it enticingly around his neck. He began to get aroused at once.

'Where to, lady?'

'Home James, and don't spare the horses . . ."'

Desmond did not need to be told twice.

Anthony Findlater made no attempt to conceal his disappointment. After the Islington warehouse in which they had been working until now, the garage seemed pokey and unsuitable. He felt hemmed in.

'We'll never be able to manage in here, David.'

'We'll have to, Ant. I just can't afford the warehouse any more. My stepfather's letting me have this rent-free. So – this is The Emperor's home from now on.' He tried to cheer his friend up. 'It won't be so bad if we leave the doors open.'

'In the winter? We'd freeze to death.'

'I'm sure we'll manage once we get used to it,' insisted David. 'Give me a hand to clear some of this stuff out of the way.'

They began to move the various items that had been stored in the garage, stacking them on shelves or tight up against the walls. Ten minutes of hard work released a few more square yards of work space and David was encouraged. He had not been able to refuse the offer of his stepfather's garage in Culross Street. His funds were so low now that he had to seize on any favours.

'And by the way,' he said. 'I owe you for two weeks.'

'Three, actually . . .'

'Let's make it a round month and I'll settle up then.'

'David, I'm sorry . . . but it can't go on like this.'

'You'll get your money, don't worry,' assured the other. 'I just happen to be a bit short at the moment.'

Anthony shuffled his feet in embarrassment. 'It's not enough.'

'What?'

'I can't get by on ten quid a week any more.'

David gaped. 'You're asking for a rise?'

'No, of course not. Look, what I'm trying to say is that . . . well, I'm going to have to take another job. We've got a lot of expenses at the moment. The flat, the baby, the au pair . . .'

'But Carole is earning as well.'

'We're still not keeping our heads above water. The simple fact is that I need to bring more money into the house.'

'So you walk out on The Emperor!' said David, angering.

'No. I work for you in the evenings, Part-time.'

'It will never be finished at that rate!'

'Sorry, but that's how it's got to be,' said Anthony with a sigh of resignation. 'I've been putting off telling you because I knew it would upset you.'

'It's certainly done that!' agreed David.

There was a pause. 'It's not what I want, believe me.'

David held him by the shoulders and looked into his eyes.

'You mustn't quit now, Ant. We've almost got it cracked. One final push now and we're there. We'll be taking The Emperor out for a test run in the New Year. Hang on till then – please!' He let his hands fall to his sides and spoke in a whisper. 'That car is all I've got between me and insanity. It's what keeps me going. It *has* to succeed. Don't you understand? The Emperor is my salvation.'

'It's too late,' said Anthony, dully.

'Too late?'

'I've accepted a job. I start work on Monday.'

David Blakely felt the ground shift beneath him.

The flat at Goodwood Court had been a much noisier place since Ruth Ellis had moved in. She liked to have loud music in the background and never seemed to be distracted by it. As she sat in her evening dress in front of the mirror in her room, the radio was blaring away nearby. She was putting the finishing touches to her appearance, going through all her little rituals in sequence. On her dressing table she had put the photograph of her daughter and another of Andrea in his school uniform. Fresh flowers stood in a vase.

Desmond, immaculate in his dress suit, peeped in through the door. She saw his reflection in the mirror.

'I won't be long. Come in.'

His first move was towards the radio which he turned down to a more civilized volume. Then he stood behind her and watched her apply a light spray of lacquer to her hair.

'Why don't you let your hair go back to its natural colour?

'No. I'm a blonde now.'

'Wouldn't you like a change?'

'Gentlemen prefer blondes.' She caught his eye in the mirror. 'And blondes prefer gentlemen. This one does, anyway.'

He picked up a small plastic box. 'I didn't know you wore false eyelashes.'

She patted the stool for him to sit beside her then she removed the false eyelashes from the box and fixed them carefully to his lids.

'They suit you, Des!'

'Don't be silly!'

'Keep still. I haven't finished yet.' She adjusted one of the lashes. 'I'll wear anything that improves on nature.' She giggled. 'Are you wondering about my teeth now?'

'I know they're real. I've seen your toothbrush in the bathroom.'

'That's just to fool you!' she teased.

She turned his head so that he could look at himself in the mirror. He smiled when he saw the effect of the false eyelashes. She studied his face very closely.

'Can I shave your moustache off, Desmond?'

'No!' he said, hiding it behind a protective hand.

Ruth laughed and turned the radio up full again.

She was awakened by the sound of a kettle being filled with water in the kitchen. Anthony had come home at last. Carole reached out for the alarm clock and angled it so that it caught some of the moonlight. It was 1.30 A.M.

She had last seen her husband when he left the house early the previous morning. The new job was turning out to have its disadvantages. Anthony brought more money into the house but he spent even less time there. He was working full-time as a second-hand car salesman and he had fallen into the habit of going straight from work to the garage in Culross Street. Carole was feeling more and more neglected. Once again, David was to blame.

There was a light tap on the door and then it inched open. Anthony had come to see if she was still awake. She closed her eyes at once and lay motionless. It was too late and she was too tired to have yet another row about The Emperor. She would see him over breakfast and they could talk then.

Her feelings about David remained ambiguous. While she held him responsible for a number of things, she still had a residual fondness for him. Since he had stopped living with Ruth Ellis in the flat above the Little Club, he had started to visit Tanza Road once more. Carole was pleased about this. It proved that he had broken his dependence on Ruth at last. For his own sake, and for the sake of his friendship with the Findlaters, David had to be kept well away from her in the future.

Carole saw it as her duty to keep them apart.

She fell asleep thinking about it.

The novelty of the classes at the Modelling School soon wore off and Ruth began to find the sessions tedious and repetitive. She had not realized how much hard work was attached to being a model. Since Desmond had paid for her, however, she persevered and kept her misgivings from him. Of all the men she had known, he was by far the easiest to handle. In moving to Goodwood Court, she had fallen on her feet and she was grateful. The least she could do to repay Desmond was to keep up her attendances at the Modelling School.

After yet another long and disappointing session, she left the building to find that heavy drizzle was falling. She put up her umbrella and was about to step out into the street when she was confronted by a pale, drawn face and wounded eyes.

'How did you find me?'

'It wasn't hard,' said David. 'Are you really living with Cussen?'

'Yes.'

'I suppose he's paying for everything?'

Panic touched her and she dashed wildly out into the road without looking where she was going. A double-decker bus braked sharply to avoid hitting her and the driver howled abuse through an open window. David picked his way more carefully through the traffic and reached the opposite pavement. He soon overhauled her.

'Go away!'

'You should invest some of Desmond's money in a guide dog and a white stick,' he suggested. 'You almost got killed just now.'

'Why should you care?'

'You know why . . .'

She tried to push past him but he held her by the arm.

'Leave me alone!'

'Do you sleep with him?'

'Yes.'

'You're disgusting.'

He let go of her and she started to shiver.

'It's cold. I want to go home.'

'Stay with me,' he pleaded.

She was torn between fear and excitement. 'Where . . .?'

'We could go to an hotel.'

'No.'

'I can't sleep without you, Ruth.'

She shook her head. 'I can't.'

'Is Desmond at home?'

'He's away till tomorrow night.'

'Can I come back with you?'

'That's really low!'

'I know. But can I come?'

Ruth said nothing. He flagged down a taxi and helped her in.

'Where to, sir?'

'She'll tell you.'

Feeling numb and helpless, Ruth gave the address.

The taxi drove off into the late afternoon gloom.

They were let out in Devonshire Street. David had no money and Ruth had to pay the fare. Before he drove away, the cabbie shot her a knowing look and her guilt stirred. She led the way into Goodwood Court and went furtively up the stairs, hoping that they would not meet anyone on the way. When the reached the safety of the flat, she locked the door behind them and leaned against it for support, her pulse racing and her breath coming in short bursts.

David went into the living room and surveyed it carefully. Still nervous and apprehensive, she came in to join him. Without taking her eyes off him, she gathered up an armful of cushions from the easy chair and the sofa then dropped them on the floor.

'Where's his bedroom?'

'I always feel like a refugee when I'm with you.'

'Does he want to marry you?'

'I think so.'

She went to the window and drew the curtains, plunging the room into virtual darkness. Unable to keep still, she came back to the cushions and began to form a bed with them.

'Has he asked you?'

'He won't ask.'

'Why not?'

'He'd be too frightened in case I turned him down.'

'And would you?'

'Get the eiderdown.'

David turned abruptly and stalked out of the room. He opened the first door off the hallway and found himself peering into Desmond's study. It was small, neat, ordered, old-fashioned, dull. A true reflection of its owner. David slammed the door shut and tried the next one. It was Desmond's bedroom. Loud music suddenly started up in the living room. A big band was featuring its brass section. David grabbed the eiderdown off the double bed and walked out.

Ruth had turned on the radiogram. She was standing in front of the empty fireplace taking off her clothes with one hand and holding a glass of Pernod in the other. David was scornful.

'How can you live here like this?'

She was down to her underwear now and was shivering.

'Come on, then,' she invited.

But he stood there brooding, the eiderdown still in his hands. Ruth went quickly to the cushions and lay back on them. He came closer and glared down at her. She offered her challenge.

'Come on. If you're going to . . .'

He dropped the eiderdown and sank to the floor. They began to kiss away a long and painful time apart.

Andrea lolled on the sofa and half-watched Muffin the Mule jigging about on television. He was in the living room of Desmond's flat and the only light, apart from the glow from the television set, came from a set of coloured ornamental lamps decorating the large Christmas tree that stood in the corner. Returning from his first term at boarding school, Andrea had been confronted with a new home, a new situation for his mother, and a new kind of Christmas. He had adapted in his usual uncomplaining way.

Left alone in the flat, he had now become more inquisitive. He began to wonder if any Christmas presents had been bought for him. Resisting the articulated antics of Muffin the Mule, he decided to search for possible hiding places where the presents might be. He began in the study, the private lair that was filled with memorabilia of Desmond's past experiences. Some of the photographs were wartime souvenirs and showed him in flying gear, standing with the rest of the crew beside a large aeroplane. A scale model of a similar aeroplane stood on the top of the desk and beside it, draped over a lamp, was an old flying helmet.

Andrea studied it all with glistening eyes but he did not forget the main purpose of his visit. He began to open the drawers of the desk and ferret about in them. No presents were found but he came upon something that took his breath away. Hidden away in one of the drawers were two handguns and a starting pistol. Andrea was transfixed. He reached in with tentative fingers and lifted up the heavier of the two guns.

Seconds later he heard the front door of the flat opening.

'Hello, we're back!' called his mother.

He hurriedly put the gun away and closed the drawer. Then he scampered back into the living room where Ruth and Desmond were taking off their coats. She nodded towards the study.

'What were you doing in there?'

'Nothing.'

'You've been looking for Christmas presents, haven't you?' She smiled at his sheepish expression. 'Hungry?'

'Yes?'

'And you?' she asked Desmond.

'I need a drink,' he said, flopping in a chair and loosening his tie.

'And me!' decided Ruth.

Andrea called after her. 'I suppose you'll want gin?'

'Brandy for me,' said Desmond.

'Are you knackered, Des?'

He frowned at the boy. 'Yes, I am. It's all this shopping.'

Anxious to please, Andrea poured him a glass of brandy from the decanter and took it over to him. Desmond raised it to him.

'Cheers!'

'Would you like a cigar?'

'Yes, please.'

'Big or little?'

'Big.'

Andrea went to the box on the coffee table and selected a large cigar. When he brought it over to Desmond, the latter ceremoniously nipped the end off it. The boy now picked up a table-lighter and struck it. He held the flame right up to the cigar and Desmond puffed away until he was certain that it was lit. Then he nodded to Andrea who snuffed out the flame.

Unseen by either of them, Ruth watched the ritual from the doorway. She swung on her heel and went back into the kitchen.

He soon realized that it had been a mistake to come. Christmas Day in Penn was a less than exciting event for David Blakely. His mother and stepfather went off for drinks with a neighbour in the morning and David repaired to The Crown for company. The pub was almost empty. When he got back to the house in the afternoon, he soon found himself alone yet again. After a big, celebratory lunch, his mother and stepfather retired to their bedroom for a rest. David was left in a huge, empty, funless, friendless house. Boredom nibbled at him.

A few hours of solitary drinking only increased his misery and he knew that he had to get away. Making his excuses, he jumped in his car and drove back to London as if he were competing at Silverstone. He headed straight for Goodwood Court and trotted up the stairs with the toy gun he had bought as a Christmas present for Andrea. After the maddening disappointments of the day so far, he had relied on Ruth to be there to cheer him up and he was mortified to learn that she had slipped out for a drink with friends. A note pinned to the door of the flat explained where she was and it sent the now frantic David reeling off to the nearest public telephone.

'How's Morrie?' asked Ruth. 'Full of the Christmas spirit?'

'Full of piss and wind more like!' said Christine.

'He doesn't change, then!'

'Oh, I know what I wanted to ask you, Ruth. What did you buy for the two men in your life? Must have been a bit awkward.'

'Not really. They both got the same thing. Identical silver cigarette cases!'

The two friends cackled happily together.

Ruth had invited Christine and her current man to a small party at Goodwood Court that night. The three of them had come out for a pre-party drink at a nearby club and the two women were catching up on each other's news with great relish.

'What happens if they offer each other a fag!' said Christine.

'I'll just have to make a run for it, darling!'

The banter was soon interrupted by the landlord. There was a telephone call for a Mrs Ellis. Ruth went off into the back room to take it and heard David's voice screaming down the line at her.

'Where the fuck are you, Ruth?'

'I was just . . .'

'On Christmas Day of all days! To walk out and leave the poor kid alone in the flat! It's downright wicked!'

'We only popped out for a quick drink . . .'

'And why wasn't *I* invited to your bloody party!'

'You said you were going down to Penn.'

'Don't mention Penn!' he yelled. 'You should be *here*, Ruth!'

'Where?'

'At Cussens' place. Andy needs you and I want you. Haven't you got any fucking consideration for other people!'

'Look, David . . .' she began, trying to pacify him.

He was beyond reason. 'God, what a lousy mother you are! When I think of what Andy has suffered because of you! And now you desert him on Christmas day so that you can guzzle some gin! It's criminal!' I ought to report you to the police! If you don't get back here right away, I will! You're not allowed to abandon kids of that age!'

Ruth was so hurt and flustered now that she had no idea what to say. David was clearly in a highly disturbed state and needed calming down. She could not bear to hear him ranting any more.

'I'm on my way!' she said and put the receiver down.

Flushed and anxious, she told the others that she had to go on ahead and she hurried back to Goodwood Court. David was sitting outside the door of the flat, sulking and vengeful. Afraid that the neighbours would hear him shouting at her, she took him inside. She tried to sedate him with apologies but he brushed them aside. All the accumulated grievances of their relationship came to the surface. David wanted a showdown.

'Why do you live in his fucking flat?' he demanded.

'Because I was kicked out of my own. Thanks to you.'

'My fault now!'

'I had a good job until you came along, David Blakely!'

'Running a brothel!'

'Nightclub!'

He panted for a few moments. 'Why did you walk out on me?'

'Because I had a better offer.'

'Cussen? That turd?'

'At least he's a real man!' she asserted. 'He looks after me. He doesn't ponce on me like you do!'

He curled his lip in contempt. 'You're nothing but his whore!'

'I'm bloody not!'

'He pays the rent, the school fees, everything. He provides the money and you provide the sex! What's that if it's not whoring?'

'You wouldn't understand!'

He took her by the shoulders. 'If you loved me, as you say you do, you couldn't bear to let that little prick touch you!'

'Jealousy! That's good coming from you!'

'What do you mean!'

'What about all the women you've fucked since you've known me?'

'Shut up!' he ordered, pushing her on the sofa.

'You know you have! My God, I've seen the way you act, David Blakey! I've *seen* you!'

SHUT UP!'

'Does she pay you for it?'

He slapped her across the face and there was a scream but it did not come from her. Awakened by their row, Andy was standing in the doorway in his pyjamas. Both of them were immediately contrite and ashamed. Ruth rushed to fold him in her arms and David mumbled apologies. The boy was taken back to his room by his mother and settled down again. She promised him that there would be no more shouting and arguing.

When she came back into the living room, however, David was ready for another slanging match. Insisting that he had never had an affair with Carole Findlater, he told her that he would take her over to Tanza Road that minute and prove it. They would confront Carole with her accusation and she would tell the truth.

'David, I can't leave *now*,' implored Ruth.

'It's important!'

'But we're having a party. People are coming.'

'We're going to sort this out once and for all, Ruth.'

'Any other time . . .'

'Now!' He took her wrist and pulled her after him.

Their bitter row continued all the way down the stairs and out into the street. When Desmond arrived in his car, he saw the two of them swearing and gesticulating at each other. Evidently, David was not fit to drive a car and Desmond was therefore alarmed when he pushed Ruth into his vehicle and shot off. Desmond followed them in case of an accident and he trailed them all the way to Tanza Road. He watched as they went up the stone steps to the house.

In his rage and urgency, David had completely forgotten that the Findlaters were not at their flat, having gone to stay with friends at Brighton for the weekend. Since he had keys to the flat, he let them both in and the row took on fresh strength. It finally burned itself out in its usual way and they fell into each other's arms.

'Let's do it in their bed!' decided Ruth.

They would be there for the whole night.

Desmond Cussen maintained his vigil in Tanza Road until almost 9 P.M. but the couple did not emerge. He drove away in a state of dejection and humiliation. As he headed back to the party at Goodwood Court, he wondered how he could explain away the sudden departure of the hostess or find the words to reassure a small boy in distress.

It had been an eventful Christmas Day for all of them.

7

Ruth Ellis returned to the flat on the following morning. She came alone and looked tired, anxious, shamefaced and defeated. In the cold light of day, her satin party dress and flashy jewellery were oddly incongruous. Andrea understood the situation well enough to go straight to his room. Desmond remained in his armchair, nursing his sense of betrayal, not daring to look at her, waiting for her lies.

She perched on the edge of the sofa and put her hands to her head for a moment. Then she looked penitently across at him.

'Sorry . . .' There was a long silence. 'How was the party?'

'We missed you.'

'David came.'

'I know.'

'He was in a state. He woke Andy with his yelling. I had to go with him to get him out of here. It was frightening, Des. You know what he's like when he's worked up.' She paused for a response but he said nothing. 'He made me get in his car and drove off.'

'Where to?'

'Out into the country somewhere.'

'The country . . .' he echoed, tonelessly.

'He was driving like a mad thing. I was terrified. He just kept going and going and going until we finally ran out of petrol. God knows where we were! Somewhere in the middle of Northamptonshire, I think. And of course, there were no garages open on Christmas night and so we were stuck.' She was telling the story as if she had rehearsed it several times. 'First thing this morning, David walked a mile or so to a farmhouse and they let him have a gallon. That got us to a garage . . .'

'What was it called?'

'I don't remember.'

'Where did you spend the night?'

'In the car.'

'Where was it parked?'

'I told you. Out in the country.'

His eyes smouldered with suppressed anger and his knuckles were white as he gripped the arms of the chair. When he finally spoke, his voice was low and hoarse.

'Out in the country . . .'

'It's the truth, Des!'

'Since when has 29 Tanza Road been out in the country?'

Her protest died on her lips. Prickly heat crept over her.

Desmond got up and stood over her. 'I was just coming back from my cocktail party at the office. You and Blakely were standing by his car, yelling at each other. He was obviously as drunk as a lord. When he drove you off, I followed you to Hampstead. He let himself into the Findlaters' place and you went with him. Contempt made him screw up his features. 'You slept with him there.'

'Des . . .'

'You're a liar, Ruth.'

Deprived of her alibi, she took refuge in tears. As she dabbed at her eyes with a handkerchief, her mind was feverishly casting around for an escape route, for an excuse that he would accept, for a means of survival. Her whole future at Goodwood Court was now at stake. When she had needed it most, he had given her a roof over her head and even allowed her son to spend Christmas there with them. Ruth knew that her behaviour was unforgivable and yet she had to have his forgiveness in order to stay.

She made a bid for his sympathy.

'I've been through absolute hell, Des . . .

'And what do you think *I've* been through?' he snarled. 'We were supposed to be having a party here last night. Remember? But you run off with that swine! And I'm stuck here with egg on my face!'

'It wasn't my fault,' she sobbed.

'Don't start blubbering again.'

'I didn't invite him here.'

'Then why did he come?'

'To see me.'

'You should have refused.'

'I couldn't.'

'Sent him away.'

'I tried.'

'Stayed here.'

'Des . . .'

'Damn it, woman, you live with *me* now!'

He was trembling with fury. She indicated the sofa beside her. Reluctantly, he sat down. Ruth grasped his hands tightly.

'I *know* I shouldn't have gone but I had to. It was the only way to calm him down. Get him away from here. Did you want your neighbours to hear that kind of language?'

'You didn't have to sleep with him, Ruth.'

'He forced me.'

'You could have rung for me to come and fetch you.'

'He wouldn't let me near the 'phone.'

'Then why didn't you just walk out?'

Fresh tears flowed. 'Because he threatened to kill himself . . .'

'I don't believe you.'

'All right!' she wailed. 'You don't believe me but that's what happened! David blackmailed me. He said that he'd commit suicide if I left the house. And he meant it. He was desperate. I've never seen him as bad as that. It was dangerous to leave him on his own.' She paused to get her breath back. 'So I stayed.'

Desmond was still regarding her with stony distrust. Ruth gave a resigned shrug, got up and moved towards the door.

'Where are you going?'

'To pack.'

'You don't have to leave,' he said, involuntarily.

Hope flickered. 'You want me to stay?'

'I like having you here.'

'And I love being here!'

He seemed embarrassed. 'Are you going to see him again?'

'No.'

'Have you told him?'

'Yes. It's all over.'

'Is that a promise?'

She sounded rueful. 'A promise to you – *and* to myself.'

'One more thing, Ruth . . .'

'Yes?'

'Don't lie to me again. Ever.'

She went back to him and put her arms gently around him.

The man waited in the shadows as the patrons streamed out of the cinema. After a short while, the commissionaire began to lock the large glass doors. The cinema staff now came out and called their goodbyes to him before disappearing into the night. One of the usherettes peeled away from the group and headed towards the shop doorway in which the man was lurking. She was a pert, vulgarly pretty girl with an aroma of cheap perfume about her and she giggled with pleasure when he stepped out to greet her with a lazy smile.

'Where's the car?' she asked, excitedly.

'Round the corner.'

'Hoped you'd come again.'

'I need to stay the night . . .'

David Blakely escorted her towards the waiting car.

Ruth Ellis lay in the bath and soaped a leg reflectively. Now that she had abandoned her hopes of becoming a model, she spent far more time hanging around the flat. A long, slow, warm restorative bath was part of her daily ritual and she always kept a glass of Pernod within reach. Recent events had taught her to count her blessings and she thought how lucky she was to have a man like Desmond. Anybody else would have thrown her out of the flat by now but his tolerance was remarkable. He was possessive in a negative way. Though he disapproved of much that she did, he could somehow not bring himself to reproach her. Though she lived in his flat and spent his money, he found it difficult to assert himself and to make demands on her.

Because she was so grateful to him, Ruth did not want to hurt him more than she had to. When she got out of the bath and dried herself, therefore, the first thing she did was to apply careful make-up to the tell-tale bruises on her arms. Desmond had to be spared those.

She slipped on a quilted housecoat, went back into the living room to replenish her drink, and switched on the radiogram. Then she flopped on the sofa and reached for a pile of magazines that he had bought for her. Flicking casually through the top one for something of interest, she came to a page that made her rigid with annoyance. Above a feature article about the lives of Russian women, wearing her horn-rimmed glasses and managing a thin smile, was a photograph of Carole Findlater.

On impulse Ruth tore the magazine viciously into pieces and scattered them over the floor. Carole's eyes, ripped away from the rest of her face, stared up from the carpet with understandable surprise.

* * *

The fog had lain like a blanket over most of southern England all day and it was starting to thicken towards evening. Driving back to London from a business visit to Wales, Desmond Cussen was making slow progress. Bad visibility was responsible for a serious accident ahead of him on the main road and he suddenly found himself stuck in traffic jam. It was almost an hour before the obstruction was cleared and he could do nothing but sit in the Zephyr, listening to the radio and cursing the weather. When he finally got on the move again, he decided to find a telephone kiosk from which he could ring Ruth to tell her how late he would be. At the next village he pulled on to the car park of a pub then walked back to the kiosk he had glimpsed through the fog. Hearing Ruth's voice would at least give him some consolation after a long and punitive journey.

But she was not there. The telephone rang and rang in the flat at Goodwood Court but nobody answered it. Ruth had said she would be at home all afternoon and evening. He made a careful note of the time then made his disgruntled way back to the car park.

London was virtually immobile. The fog was so heavy in some areas that buses had to be guided by men walking in front of them with burning torches. Cars and taxis inched along with blazing headlights and angry horns conversed everywhere. Extra police tried to ease the chaos. Delays and cancellations were the norm at railway stations. Only the Underground triumphed.

In weather that had sent most pedestrians hurrying home, Ruth Ellis waited near a bridge. She was wrapped up against the cold and the damp but the tall figure who came towards her out of the gloom wore only a sports coat, flannels and open-necked shirt. He touched her. No words were spoken. They felt their way down a flight of stone steps and walked along the Embankment. He could not wait.

In the anonymity of the fog, standing up against a wall, they began to make love.

She had been to Warlington Park hospital before and she was instantly reminded of her previous visit. Her husband, George, had been a patient there, undergoing treatment to cure his alcoholism. Ruth had been pregnant with their daughter at the time and in an over-wrought condition. When someone teased her that her husband was having an affair with an attractive female doctor, she flew into a jealous rage and stormed into the hospital to accuse George of being an adulterer. Ruth had been so violent that she had had to be restrained and given sedatives.

Reminded of the incident now, and of the many traumas of her marriage to George Ellis, she felt even more depressed. The weight of her past miseries pressed down on her and she began to wish that she had not come to the hospital. But it had become necessary. With the New Year still in its infancy, she had been referred as an out-patient. Fluctuating wildly between extremes, her relationship with David Blakely was telling on her more and more.

Ruth needed help.

She went into the hospital to keep her appointment with a consultant psychiatrist.

The Emperor stood disconsolately in a corner. With its engine stripped down, its wheels off and its bodywork only rudimentary, it looked skeletal and neglected. Because the garage in Culross Street had proved unsatisfactory, it had been moved to a new home, the garage where Clive Gunnell worked. A big advantage of the move was that Clive was able to help Anthony from time to time.

They arrived one evening for another session and were

soon hard at it. The telephone interrupted them. Wiping his hand on his dungarees, Anthony picked up the receiver.

'Hello . . .'

'Ant? Is that you?' gasped a voice.

'David?'

'Please come and get me!' he whined. 'Please come and get me.'

'Where are you?'

'The bitch has got my keys . . .'

David sounded as if he was struggling with someone. Anthony then heard the raw screech of Ruth's voice coming down the line.

'Where are you, David?'

'Cussen's flat . . . She won't let me drive away.' His desperation intensified. 'Please come soon, Ant. Please!'

'We're on our way . . .'

They left the garage at once.

When they got to Goodwood Court, they raced up the stairs, uncertain about what they might find at the top. The door to the flat had been left ajar and they went straight in to find David cowering in a corner while Ruth hurled abuse at him. She seemed to be standing awkwardly on one foot and her eye had been punched so hard that it was darkening and closing. Both of them were drunk and aggressive and hysterical.

Ruth greeted the newcomers.

'Fuck off!'

'Thank God you've come!' snivelled David. 'The bitch tried to knife me. Keep her away, Ant! She'll kill me!'

'Now, calm down, the pair of you!' ordered Anthony.

'You ought to be ashamed of yourselves!' reinforced Clive.

'She started it,' argued David.

'Liar!' she screamed.

'Look, that's enough!' warned Anthony.

Clive took charge. 'First thing you need is to have that eye bathed, Ruth. Where's the bathroom?'

'That bastard punched me!' she accused.

'Come on . . .'

He led her into the bathroom and saw how badly she was hobbling. One of her ankles had been injured during the fight. When he had found some cotton wool, he bathed her eye gently. Very slowly, some of her ire began to seep away.

David, meanwhile, seeing a chance to retrieve his keys, grabbed them from her handbag and bolted for the door. When Ruth came out of the bathroom and saw that he was gone, her fury was rekindled and she hobbled down the stairs after him. To stop him escaping from her, she got into the driving seat of his car.

Unable to flee in his own vehicle, David promptly dived into the other one with Anthony and Clive but Ruth was equal to this new strategy. Putting a hand through the open window of their car, she snatched the ignition key and the engine cut out. David immediately began to revile her but the other men silenced him. They both saw that the only way out of the predicament was to soothe and distract Ruth not to inflame her even more.

'You shouldn't have hit her, David!' said Anthony.

'Only a swine would beat up a woman,' agreed Clive.

'It's not the first time,' she pointed out.

'Why do you bother with him?' asked Clive.

'Good question!' she sneered.

Clive continued to placate her and sympathize with her and David saw his opportunity. Sneaking quietly away to his own car, he got in, locked the doors, then started up the engine and roared away down the street. It happened so quickly that Ruth was caught off guard. She limped after him waving a fist but she knew that she had lost. Fatigue and pain caught up with her.

'Forget him!' advised Anthony. 'He's not worth it.'

'Little shit!' she muttered.

'You need to wind down, Ruth,' said Clive. 'Come on. We'll take you for a coffee. Ant is right. Forget him . . .'

They took her to a cafe in Great Portland Street.

Carole Findlater peeled the shirt off his back and examined his wounds. He was covered in livid scratches. She made him sit on a chair while she fetched the iodine then she bent down to attend to him.

'When *will* you learn, David?' she sighed.

'She pulled a knife on me!' he whimpered.

'You're an idiot to have anything to do with her! You know how violent she gets when she's provoked.'

'But I didn't provoke her.'

'Honestly, David, you're so weak! She does the most terrible things and you always go crawling back to her.'

'Not this time,' he vowed.

'You've got nothing in common with her. She's a gutter rat. She always will be.' Carole poured the iodine on to a swab. 'You've just got to get rid of her!'

'I already have, Carole.'

'For good!'

'Tonight was it. The finish.'

She was sceptical. 'Until the next time . . .'

The iodine stung badly and he winced at the pain.

He had known it for some time but had never brought himself to admit it. Now that he had the proof, he could deceive himself no longer. It had been scrunched up in the wastepaper basket in his desk. When he had gone to empty the basket, he had noticed the distinctive yellow paper and taken a closer look at it. The bill for the Rodney Hotel had been for two people. Ruth had paid. Desmond's stomach turned.

He poured himself a brandy and sat down to wait.

When Ruth crept into the flat several hours later,

Desmond was still there, fully dressed and stretched out in the chair with the brandy decanter on the floor nearby. He woke as she entered. His face was ashen with exhaustion.

Ruth trotted out her excuse but he did not hear it.

'You've been with Blakely.'

'No, I haven't!' she denied.

Desmond took the hotel bill from his pocket and held it up. Her defiance gave way to fear which in turn was replaced by a weary resignation. Ruth sat down heavily on the sofa.

'Dated last Wednesday,' he noted. 'When you were supposed to be up north. Was it the same hotel tonight?'

She shook her head. 'Where did you find it?'

'Where you put it for me to find . . .'

Both of them knew that they would reach this point sooner or later but now that they had got there, neither of them could find the words that came next. For what seemed like an age, they just sat there in a kind of bruised silence.

Desmond was the first to break it.

'I thought you'd finished with him.'

'He got in touch.'

'But he hit you. Gave you that black eye.'

'He always comes back.'

'Have you been seeing a lot of him?'

'Yes.'

'Where?'

'Hotels. The Rodney, usually.'

'And here?' he was anxious to know. 'While I was away?'

'Yes.'

'Not fair . . .' he murmured. 'Has he hit you again?'

'You know what he's like when he's had too much to drink. He doesn't know what he's doing.'

'That's no excuse!' he snapped.

'No . . .'

There was another long silence. This time she ended it.

'I'd better move out of here. It's not right for me to stay any more.'

'Why can't you tell him once and for all to stay away?'

'Desmond, you've been so good to me and Andy . . .'

'Don't tell me how good I've been!' he exploded.

'I should never have come here after I left the Club.'

'I asked you to come.'

'I'll move out, anyway.'

'Where to?'

'Who knows?' she said, wearily. 'At the rate I'm going, I'll end up in a Salvation Army Hotel if I'm not careful.'

He studied her face. 'You look terrible.'

'So do you.' She gave a dry laugh. 'Maybe we should go to bed and wait there till the psychiatrist comes!'

'Maybe . . .'

It was a large, gloomy, genteely decaying mansion block in Egerton Gardens. Framed against the dark clouds it looked dignified but uninviting. The bedsitter was small and airless and reached by a climb up a flight of stairs. As before, Desmond was a willing beast of burden, struggling with the bulk of the luggage while Ruth confined herself to a few special items. One of them was a huge bunch of carnations in a cellophane wrapper, a present from Desmond. He was attentive without being intrusive and was determined not to outstay his welcome.

'I must be off, Ruth . . .'

'Thanks for everything, Des.' She sniffed the flowers. 'Especially these. They're gorgeous!'

'I'll find a vase,' offered the landlady.

'I'd appreciate that,' said Ruth.

'And if there's anything else you need, Mrs Ellis, you only have to ask.'

The old lady gave her a polite smile and went out.

'I'll see you later, Ruth.' said Desmond.

'Bye . . .'

He left the room quickly in order to catch the landlady up on the stairs. Seeing that he wanted a word with her, she paused halfway down. Desmond produced a card from his wallet and gave it to her without formality.

'This is my card. I'm Mrs Ellis's closest friend,' he impressed upon her. 'If anything crops up, illness or anything, just get in touch with me at once. You've got my office number and my home number there.'

She glanced at the visiting card and nodded. Desmond raised his hat to her and carried on down the stairs. At the bottom he remembered something else and turned to call up to her.

'I'll be around a fair bit to see how she's getting on.'

He went out to the Zephyr, got in and looked up at the building. Misgivings surfaced at once. He drove swiftly away.

The laundrette was a long narrow room which had two rows of machines facing each other menacingly like gun-slingers in a shoot-out. Every so often one of them would fire off noisily and vibrate all over. There was a row of chairs bolted together and a lone poster that emphasized the bareness of the rest of the wall. The place was cold, impersonal and functional.

A late afternoon in February found it crowded with bustling women and boisterous children and the occasional smack was being given away free by the former. The only man who was there sat reading a newspaper and tried to ignore the general tumult as washing steamed, thumped and sloshed around or spun dizzily in the driers.

Ruth Ellis was having to get used to the Laundrette. While she had been living at Goodwood Court, she had enjoyed the luxury of a collect and deliver laundry service. Along with many other comforts that she had taken for granted, that had now vanished. Ruth was in the process of emptying her drier, carefully removing the clothes one by one and folding them with meticulous concern before putting them into her bag. The exercise was designed to cut down on the ironing but it only sharpened the impatience of the woman who was waiting to use the drier.

The door of the laundrette opened and David Blakely came in. When he walked over to Ruth, she gave him a noncommital look and carried on with what she was doing.

'I thought I'd find you here,' he said.

She handed him the end of a sheet and he helped to fold it up neatly with her. Impatience increased at Ruth's elbow.

'Are you going to monopolize this machine much longer?'

'Cut-throat places these laundrettes, aren't they?' observed David with distaste.

'I hate them,' said Ruth.

The woman's exasperation was showing clearly. 'Just empty everything out and fold it up over there,' she urged, pointing to the large table at the far end of the room. 'That's what it's for.'

'Don't be too harsh on my mother, madam,' apologized David with an ironic smirk. 'She isn't used to doing her own washing.'

'Why aren't you at work?' asked Ruth.

'I wanted to see you so I finished early and drove down.'

'If you keep doing impulsive things like that, you'll get into trouble again,' she warned in a neutral tone.

'Silicon Pistons can manage without me for an afternoon.'

'As long as your stepfather doesn't find out.'

'I can handle him,' he said, airily.

Ruth took the last item of washing out of the drier and

began to fold it. The impatient woman pounced in triumph on the machine. David watched Ruth as she packed her bag. She seemed rather subdued and distracted.

'You look very pretty. New hairstyle?'

'I had it done this morning.'

'I sometimes think you're having a love affair with your hairdresser. You seem to spend all your time there.' He picked up the bag of washing. 'Shall we go to the pictures tonight? Or would you rather eat?'

'Can't we do both?'

'How much money have you got?'

'Not much.'

They moved to the door and he held it open for her.

'What's up?' he asked. 'Missing Andy?'

'A bit,' she admitted. 'He seems so little to be living away from home on his own.'

They went out of the laundrette and strolled to where he had parked the car. David stowed the washing into the boot. Ruth stood beside the vehicle with one hand on the bonnet.

'I'm pregnant,' she said.

He was not sure how to react. They got into the car and he started up the engine. He had parked in between a truck and a small van and the car needed to be manoeuvred carefully out. David gave the task all his concentration. They had driven for a couple of minutes before Ruth spoke again.

'Shall I have an abortion?'

'No.'

'Why not? One more won't make any difference now?'

'Don't talk like that.'

'You don't exactly seem bowled over by the news.'

The car soon pulled up outside the mansion block in Egerton Gardens. They got out and walked towards the entrance, David carrying the washing and Ruth fumbling in her handbag for the key. As they climbed the steps to the front door, she turned to him.

'I wish you were pleased with it.'

'I am.'

'Is that the truth, David?'

'Of course. There's nothing to stop us getting married now, is there?'

Her spirits lifted. 'No. Nothing.'

'There we are then . . .'

'Do you really mean it?'

He embraced her gently and she leaned against him. With great tenderness, he raised a hand to touch her hair.

'This time next year we can all be together,' he promised. 'Andy, too.'

'That would be lovely, wouldn't it?' she said, softly.

They went into the dark empty hall and climbed the stairs.

8

It was still quite early when Anthony Findlater arrived at the garage. Curtains were still closed in most of the upstairs windows in the road. A delivery boy cycled past him, stuffed a Sunday newspaper through the letterbox of a door, then rode on around the corner. Church bells were ringing somewhere in the distance. There was a hint of rain.

He let himself into the garage, switched on the lights and crossed over to the car to remove the tarpaulin that covered it. A shock awaited him. David Blakely was sitting in The Emperor. He was wrapped up in an old overcoat and his long scarf had been wound several times around his neck. He was fast asleep.

Anthony was startled.

'What's going on!'

David awoke slowly and painfully, rubbing his eyes with his knuckles and yawning uncontrollably. An involuntary shiver went through him.

'What in God's name are you doing here, David?'

'Competing in the Belgian Grand Prix.'

'Be serious.'

'I am, Ant. If you hadn't dragged me out of my dream, I'd have overtaken the Maserati and won.' He yawned again. 'I'm shagged out.'

'Haven't you got anywhere else to sleep?'

'This is the one place I don't get nagged.'

'Don't count your chickens,' warned Anthony. 'Do you realize you owe me five weeks' wages.'

'You know you'll get it,' said David, dismissively.

'When?'

'When I'm in a position to pay you . . .'

'You always say that.'

Anthony started to put on the dungarees. David got out of the car and stretched himself. His eyes were hollow, his skin pale and his mouth unpleasantly dry. A night curled up in The Emperor had left him aching in every joint.

'Sold many cars this week?'

'Two.'

David tapped The Emperor. 'This bloody thing would be finished by now if we didn't have to work part-time on it.'

'She's coming along,' encouraged the other.

'She'll have to come along a bit faster.'

'Why?'

'I've entered her in a race at Oulton Park on April the 2nd.'

'She's not ready for that, David.'

'She'll have to be.'

Anthony shrugged, picked up his tool-kit and went around to the other side of the car. David slipped off his coat. The both of them began work on the engine.

'What's panicked you?' asked Anthony.

'Nothing.'

'I'm not blind, David.'

'Nothing.'

'Is it that bloody woman again?'

David heaved a sigh. 'She's pregnant.'

'Who's the father? Anyone she knows?'

'Don't talk about her like that. It's mine.'

'How would you know?'

'Because I do, that's why!' snapped David.

'But Cussens pays her rent, doesn't he? He must still be . . .'

'The child is *mine*!' he howled. 'IT'S MINE!'

Anthony threw down the spanner and started to take

off his dungarees. David's anger evaporated at once. Concern took over.

'What are you doing?'

'What does it look like?'

'Ant . . .'

'Get stuffed!'

He put the dungarees under his arm and moved to the door.

'Where are you going?'

'Home.'

'What about the car?'

'Sod the car!'

David chased after him and implored him to stay but it was all to no avail. Tolerant and easy-going as a rule, Anthony had been caught on the raw by David's vicious outburst. There was a limit to what he would put up with and David had gone beyond it.

Grim and silent, Anthony drove back home.

Half an hour later, the two men were at the flat in Tanza Road. Anthony was still nursing his hurt feelings and David was cradling a glass of brandy in his hands and trying to find an apology that would be accepted. Carole watched him without sympathy.

David looked from one to the other.

'You and Carole are the best friends I've got, Ant. The *only* friends in some ways. I don't want to quarrel with you.'

Carole was blunt. 'As long as you're involved with that woman, you'll be quarrelling with everybody.'

'She's going to have my baby,' said David, simply.

'It could be Cussen's kid,' argued Anthony.

'He hasn't got it in him!' sneered the other.

'It *could* be,' repeated Anthony. 'Use your common-sense, David. You're not stupid enough to let her black-mail you with the oldest trick in the book.'

'She's had a rough life . . .'

'Don't give me that sob story,' said Carol, contemptuously. 'We've all had rough lives one way or another. If you marry her, then she'll drag you down to her level because she's incapable of rising to yours. You've only got to look at the woman!'

David shrugged. 'I like the look of her.'

Carole curled her lip in derision.

'As long as she stays in her own class, she's all right,' said Anthony. 'But put her in yours and you know damn well she just won't fit in. How do you think your mother would get on with her?'

'And your stepfather,' reinforced Carole. 'They'd die with shame!'

'She's bad news, David.'

Carole was more scornful. 'She's pure disaster!'

David put a hand to his forehead and tried to hold in the demons. He was cornered, bewildered, afraid. It was a state that Ruth Ellis had driven him into more than once.

'What shall I do?' he asked.

'Flush her out of your life!' advised Carole.

Anthony agreed. 'If you've entered The Emperor in a race at Oulton Park in April, worry about that. Not her.'

David crossed over to the window and looked down into the street. When he was with them, he felt that they were right, but something held him back from taking their advice. It was a compound of love, fear and compulsion. Ruth had a strange power over him and he had not learned to resist it.

He sounded utterly dejected.

'Maybe I should hire a bodyguard to keep her away from me.'

'You don't need a bodyguard,' urged Carole. 'She's a very little woman, David. You've just let her get out of hand.'

When he left Tanza Road, his mind was made up.

* * *

Ruth Ellis banged on the doors of the garage until they shook. She put on her glasses and stood on tiptoe so that she could peer through the tiny window. It was dark inside. All she could make out was the shape of The Emperor under her tarpaulin. Convinced that David was hiding in there somewhere, she beat another loud tattoo on the doors and only broke off when her fists were too sore.

Desmond Cussen sat in his car and watched her.

There was nothing else he could do.

A log fire burned in the grate. Brass and glass gleamed all around and caught the flicker of the yellow flames. Faces glowed in the firelight and the atmosphere was warm, cosy and companionable. The lounge bar of The Crown had attracted a lot of custom that evening. Landlord and staff were having to work hard. Seats were at a premium.

David Blakely had arrived early enough to secure a table near the fire. He was part of a group that contained Carole and Anthony Findlater, the woman whom he often visited at her house in Penn, and a few local friends. David was showing off in front of the woman and boasting about The Emperor. Anthony loyally supported him. Both men had now come to feel that the car really would be an instant success. Everybody at the table was drinking happily and feeling mellow.

Then Ruth Ellis arrived.

Quivering with rage, she made straight for David.

'I knew you'd either be in here drinking yourself stiff, or hiding up your nanny's skirt at the ancestral home, you gutless cretin! You thought you were safe here surrounded by all these toffee-nosed twats who think the sun shines out of your porthole, didn't you?'

All conversation had been killed. People either shuddered with embarrassment or watched with ghoulish fascination. The landlord came round from behind the bar and waved an admonishing hand.

'Now come on, madam . . .'

Ruth was still glaring at David. 'I suppose they're all under the false impression that you've got a shred of decency in your body!'

'Enough of that,' warned the landlord, intervening.

'Keep your nose out of it before I bite the bloody thing off!' she snarled at him. 'I didn't come all this way to have a word with you. It's him I'm after!'

She lunged at David but he dodged away.

'You cowardly, two-faced treacherous mockery of a man!' she ranted. 'If you don't want to have anything to do with me, I wish you had the nerve to say it to my face, then I wouldn't be so ashamed of ever having had anything to do with you!'

David looked apologetically at the other customers. 'I'm sorry about this . . . she's . . .'

'Who's with this lady?' demanded the landlord.

Desmond Cussen came tentatively forward from the doorway.

'Can you get her out of here?'

Desmond nodded and moved in closer to Ruth who was still trying to hit David. The latter was making sure that others stood between him and the now hysterical woman who had lost all control.

'All you're interested in is number one. When you're in trouble, you expect the whole bleeding world to rally round and bale you out. But let anybody *need* you and you're not seen for dust!' She flailed her arms at him and he stepped back. 'You're so shit-scared you turn my stomach over . . . Haven't you got the guts to say goodbye to my face?'

Desmond tried to take her arm but she shook him away. David now made his way towards the door and she followed vengefully.

'Everything about you stinks of hypocrisy and fear, and I don't know which smells the most disgusting . . .'

'Get her out before I call the police,' said the landlord.

'She's going, she's going,' assured Desmond.

A whole group of them had now moved towards the door and when David made a sudden dash through it, and Ruth darted after him, the others spilled out on to the car park. They ringed the combatants.

'You're scum, David Blakely!' she shouted.

He avoided her fist and retaliated by yelling at Desmond.

'You're devoted to her, aren't you, Cussen? You'll drive her all this way out of London just to let her make a fool of herself. You're a real friend!' he said, sarcastically. 'You'll be making her dresses and bleaching her hair for her soon.'

'Fucking pig!' she shrieked.

He caught her wrists as she dived at him.

'Take her, Cussen!' he bellowed. 'Now you've chauffeured her here, you can chauffeur her straight back.'

Ruth sank her teeth into David's hand then clawed at his cheeks. Losing his temper, he bunched a fist and punched her hard in the face. She staggered back and Desmond supported her for a moment. Then he himself went for David, grabbing him by the lapels and letting his hatred of the man explode into flame at last.

'What about hitting a man instead of a woman for a change?'

'I wouldn't bother hitting *you*!' retorted David.

'Aren't you man enough for that even?'

'Crawl back to London where you came from, Cussens!'

Desmond struck him once and David immediately backed away, hiding behind Anthony for protection and gibbering with fear. Since Ruth was obviously still dazed, Desmond decided that his first priority must be to get her away. Shepherding her to the Zephyr, he helped her in then went quickly around to the driving seat.

They were soon speeding away from Penn.

People started to move back into the pub to discuss it all over a drink. David felt a consoling arm around his shoulder.

'Come on, old son,' said Anthony.

'I didn't know she was like this . . .'

The landlady went slowly up the stairs and knocked on the door. When there was no reply, she put an ear to the wood and listened. Loud music from within suggested that someone was there. She knocked more firmly and the music soon quietened a little. Then the door swung open and Ruth Ellis, in slippers and dressing gown, confronted her.

'Good morning, Mrs Ellis. These just came for you.'

'For me?'

David Blakely had sent her some red carnations.

She took one out and stroked the bruise on her face.

Desmond Cussen was dictating a letter when the telephone call came. He motioned his secretary out of the room so that he could talk in private. Ruth sounded tired and depressed. He had arranged to take her out for a meal that evening and had been looking forward to it all week. Ruth was ringing to cry off. She was feeling unwell and had decided to have an early night. Hiding his disappointment under a show of concern, Desmond offered to call round to see her and asked if there was anything he could bring. While assuring him that she would love to see him, Ruth told him that she would prefer it if he came the next day instead. She was simply not up to receiving visitors.

Desmond wondered if that included David Blakely.

'Have you heard from him?'

'No. And I'm not likely to after our little dust-up at his

local. I certainly put a spoke in his wheel!' she said with a snort of pleasure. 'His stepfather must have heard about it and that won't have done Mr Blakely one bit of good!'

'Would you take him back if he asked?'

'He won't.'

'But if he did?'

There was a pause. 'I'll see you tomorrow, Des . . .'

She put the receiver down and consigned him to a bleak evening.

Heavy rain was drumming on the top of the car. Rivulets ran down the windows, making it impossible to see out. When a van swished past, all he saw was the glow of its headlights. High heels clicked on the pavement and the passenger door opened. Ruth lowered her umbrella and clambered in, pulling the door shut after her. Her raincoat was glistening and her boots darkened by moisture.

'You should have let me come to your room,' he said.

'Spot of rain never hurt anyone.' She looked at him more closely and caught a whiff of his breath. 'Did you drive in that state?'

'I got here, didn't I?'

'You drink too much, David.'

'Look who's talking!'

He leaned over and slipped a hand inside her raincoat to fondle her breast. She immediately pushed him away.

'I wouldn't have bothered coming out in this weather if I'd known it was only for this.'

'You knew exactly what you were coming out for, Mrs Ellis.'

Ruth tried to open the door but he restrained her.

'Would you like to hit me again?' she said, defiantly.

'You ask for it.'

'And I damn well get it, don't I?' She clicked her tongue. 'I keep hoping you'll change but you never do.'

'I can't help it.'

'You don't carry on like this with other people. You're scared shitless of letting them see what you're really like.'

'You're no better,' he argued. 'We both stink to high heaven!'

David let go of her and sat back. She fumbled for the switch above her head and put on the interior light so that she could see him more clearly. He looked rough, unshaven, hunted. A fallen angel. She thrust her hand into her handbag and took something out for him. It was a small Jeweller's box. David opened it and saw a tiny gold charm in the shape of a racing car.

He was touched by the gift.

'My good luck charm . . .'

He gently pulled the scarf from her head and opened her coat at the neck. A small silver crucifix was revealed.

'I see you're still wearing yours,' he noted.

'To protect me against Devils and Vampires.'

He switched the light off then felt for her in the dark.

'I can't see you,' he whispered.

'I don't want to be seen.'

For a while, she resisted him.

Morris Conley paid his usual visit to the Little Club to keep a fatherly eye on the hostesses and a beady one on the takings. He found time for a chat with Christine and learned something which made his eyebrows shoot up in astonishment.

'Getting married? Ruth?'

'She rang me earlier this week,' said the barmaid.

'But she hasn't got rid of that lush of a husband yet.'

'She has, Morrie. Almost, anyway. It's final next month.'

'Out of the frying pan into the bloody fire!' he mused. 'Ruth never changes, does she? Who's the lucky geyser?'

'Can't you guess?'

Conley's jaw dropped. 'Not that stupid sod of a racing

driver! Ruth wants her head examined. He was the reason I had to sling her out of here.' Bitter memories flooded back. 'Before that sponger rolled up, wc were taking two hundred quid a week here. Then Ruth starts letting him have free drinks and hand-outs and suddenly I'm finding only eighty or ninety quid in the till.'

'You don't need to tell me, Morrie. I saw it happen. Night after night.' The barmaid sighed. 'And she still thinks he's going to marry her . . .'

'Well, isn't he?'

'I'd be very surprised. Ruth says he's promised to set the date after he's driven in some big race with his new car. That was the deal. She had to get off his back so he could finish the car . . .'

'Then Lover Boy comes through with a proposal on his bended knee . . .'

'Something like that.'

'And Ruth *believed* him?' he gasped.

Christine nodded sadly. 'Yes. She sounded so excited over the 'phone. Been ringing up all her friends to tell them. I didn't have the heart to suggest that he might be stringing her along.'

'Women!' sneered Conley. 'Sometimes I think they're born stupid.'

'We are, Morrie. That's why we work for you.'

He chuckled richly and bought her a drink.

Bright sunlight brought large crowds to watch the motor racing at Oulton Park. The stands were full, expectations were high, and the general air of nervous excitement helped to key up the drivers. Race conditions were excellent and lap times threatened existing records. The motor racing fraternity was there in force and the big names were scattered liberally among the unknowns and the hopefuls.

David Blakely was in a state of anticipatory delight. By

dint of hard work and long overtime, he and Ant had somehow managed to get the Emperor ready for its debut and it was looking magnificent. He had every confidence in the machine and was impatience itself as he waited for his turn on the track.

Ruth had driven up to Chester with David and Ant that morning. Carole met them at Oulton Park and although there was still friction between the two women, it was subdued by their common desire to see The Emperor justify itself. When David's race finally arrived, he got into the car and revved the engine dramatically. Standing near the exhaust, Ruth was forced to jump away.

'I need a smog mask to stand there!' she giggled.

'Wish me luck!' said David.

'All the best my darling!' Ruth kissed him.

'Good luck, David!' called Carole.

Ant slapped the car affectionately. 'Don't let us down, old girl!'

Drivers were now being called to the starting grid. David pulled down his glasses and sent The Emperor gliding out on to the track. The booming voice over the public address system introduced the competitors to the crowd. Ruth cheered loudly when David's name was mentioned and Ant raised crossed fingers in hope. Everything was riding on The Emperor's performance. It had to do well.

When the flag sent them haring away, David immediately joined the leading half-dozen cars and stayed with them. He was driving as if his life depended on winning, taking the most daring risks and escaping disaster time and again by a matter of inches. He was fourth, then third, then second, then third again, then second once more. Down the home strait, he actually got his nose in front of the leader for a split-second. Ant and Ruth were delirious with joy and even Carole was shouting encouragement.

The Emperor was performing with imperial power.

Then tragedy intervened.

As David mounted another assault on the leader, he called for maximum thrust from the car and swung on the driving wheel to overtake. Too much had been asked of The Emperor too soon. With a resounding bang, the engine exploded and David felt the accelerator go dead. Groans of sympathy went up from the spectators and the course commentator pronounced sentence. David was out of the race. After years of dreaming and month after month of hard work on the car, he was now rolling back impotently towards the pits. It was a catastrophe.

Someone had to be blamed for it.

'Are you satisfied now?' he yelled at Ruth, as he hauled himself out of the crippled car. 'If you'd allowed me to concentrate instead of hounding me while I was working on her, this wouldn't have happened! You're a jinx, Mrs Ellis!' He kicked a front wheel in anguish. 'Well, that's the end of it now. I'll have to sell her!'

'It's only teething trouble,' soothed Anthony.

'You can't just give up,' added Carole.

David was inconsolable. 'Everything depended on winning today. There's no more money.'

'We'll get some,' announced Ruth.

'Where from? he asked.

'Your stepfather isn't exactly bare-arsed skint . . .'

David went almost berserk. Suddenly overwhelmed by her gall and by her ready assumptions, he grabbed her by the neck and held her facing the track along which cars were still screaming only feet away from them.

'You are so bloody stupid!' he roared. 'You think all I've got to do is hold my hand out while the old man pours money into it, don't you? Let me tell you about the old man. He insists on giving me an allowance, and he makes me beg for my allowance by forgetting to give it to me regularly. He thinks I'm nothing!' He squeezed her neck more tightly. 'The Emperor's finished now because I'm not crawling round him any more!'

He thrust her away from him towards the track. For a moment it seemed as if she might be knocked flying by one of the cars that flashed past. Carole screamed in fear. Ant jumped forward and pulled Ruth back to safety. She was petrified.

The optimistic journey north now gave way to a miserable return to London. A potential race-winning car went home as a signal failure. It was much more than just a mechanical disaster. When the engine blew up at Oulton Park so did Ruth's hopes of marriage to David. The Emperor was a fitting symbol of their relationship. Sad, wounded and pitiable, it was being towed away in disgrace.

Unable to stay awake, Andrea lay on his mother's bed and drifted asleep. Desmond pulled a blanket over him then returned to the window to stare out into the night. The boy's trunk was open on the floor with his golliwog and toys uppermost. These few playthings looked more tattered then ever.

It was another hour before a key turned in the lock.

Ruth's anxiety was stilled when she saw her son.

'Thank God, he's all right! I completely forgot he was coming home . . . I was so involved with Georgina, I missed the train back.'

'And how is she?' asked Desmond, levelly.

'She's beautiful, Des. I could hardly bear to leave her.'

He studied her. 'You haven't been to visit your daughter . . .'

'Yes, I have,' she faltered.

'Andy's Headmaster telephoned your landlady to find out what was happening to the lad in the holidays. She phoned me because, as far as she knew, you'd gone off with your husband, Mr Ellis, to the races.'

Guilt whitened her face. 'I'm sorry . . .

In order not to disturb Andrea, Desmond took her outside. He spoke in urgent whispers and left her in no doubt about his disgust.

'Why in Christ's name doesn't he leave you alone? All he's interested in is himself. Blakely doesn't give a damn about anybody else.'

'I know,' she accepted.

'What about Andy? He'd have been on his own all night if I hadn't been here. Doesn't Blakely think about things like that? A child alone all night? The whole thing's filthy, Ruth!' He was seething with anger at the injustice of it all. 'While he's treating you as though you're a tart, a kiddie's left to fend for himself. It isn't right!'

Ruth had no defence. She talked with candour.

'When David asked me to watch The Emperor race, I just went . . .'

'And nothing else mattered.'

'No.'

'Not even your son?'

'I forgot.'

'How could you?'

'I just did. I had something else on my mind.'

'Blakely.'

'Yes . . .'

Desmond spat the next words out. 'I'm sick of seeing you on your knees to a man who treats you like dirt! . . . Has he been hitting you again?'

'I don't know.'

'Even you must know when somebody beats the living daylights out of you!' he said, almost shouting.

'Please don't . . .'

'And look at you now. Like a ghost.'

'It's been a bad day. I feel rough.'

'Who's fault is that?'

She nodded towards the room. 'Where will Andrea sleep?'

'I've arranged to borrow a camp bed from the landlady.'

Ruth went back into the room and sat on the edge of the bed to gaze down on her son. Desmond stood at her shoulder.

'I wanted it to be better,' she whispered. 'I had a rotten childhood, Des. Always on the move. Dad thumping us. No money, no fun, no nothing. I wanted it to be *better* for my kids. I really did.' She gestured helplessly. 'What went wrong?'

'I'll get the camp bed for Andy . . .'

'I feel as if my brain is trying to jump out of my head.'

Desmond watched her then went quietly out.

When the camp bed was brought and erected, Andy was transferred to it with some difficulty. Ruth was evidently in pain and Desmond offered to call a doctor but she would not hear of it. Thanking him for all his help, she saw him out and then went straight to bed.

She slept fitfully for a couple of hours.

When she awoke the room was still pitch dark. The pain seemed distant at first but it soon approached at speed. Ruth was bent double by the racking agony. She reached down to find herself lying in a pool of blood. Fighting against the throbbing torment of the pain, she struggled to throw back the sheets and get out of bed. She put her feet to the ground, balanced on them for a second and then pitched forward into oblivion.

The bang woke Andy up and he came over to her at once. She lay small and twisted on the floor, spreading her stain all over the carpet. Andy opened the door and blundered out in search of help.

Desmond Cussen packed the presents into a carrier bag then checked his appearance in the mirror. He left his flat, got in the Zephyr, and began the journey to Egerton Gardens. It was the morning of Good Friday and religion was making its mark on London. As he drove along the now familiar route, he wished once again that they had found somewhere other than Egerton Gardens for Ruth. It was uncomfortably close to the Little Club and to the Hyde Park Hotel. She needed to get far away from the area and its distressing associations.

Ruth's miscarriage had come as a great shock to him. But he had adapted to the situation with typical readiness. He was helping to nurse her back to full fitness. She was drawing strength from him and this pleased him immensely. He was needed again.

He turned into Egerton Gardens and came within sight of the mansion block. Something caused him to alter his plans and to drive on past the building. David Blakely's car was parked outside.

The room was now spotlessly tidy. The camp bed had been folded neatly away and Andrea's toys stacked in a box. Clean sheets were on the bed. Ruth sat in front of a two-bar electric fire gazing ahead of her. An unopened magazine lay on her lap. A cigarette burned in an ashtray.

There was a knock on the door.

She opened it to admit David. He was wearing a suit and carrying a massive bunch of red carnations, a chocolate Easter Egg and a flat package. When he offered her the flowers, she ignored them. He came into the room and put them on the bed. Ruth sat down again.

'Are you all right now?' he enquired.

'I'm still bleeding. Otherwise I'm as fit as a fiddle.'

David was uneasy in the room . . . He kept shifting his feet and glancing around as if expecting someone to come in.

'Why are you here?' she asked.

'You've been trying to get hold of me all week.'

'So your friend did tell you I phoned?'

'Yes.'

'But you didn't bother to call me back?'

'I've been busy.' He ran his tongue over his lips. 'I'm sorry about the baby.'

'Weren't you interested in knowing how I was?'

'I didn't like thinking about it. It was mine, too, you know.'

'I see,' she observed, tartly. 'Now that it's safely out of the way, it's your baby again and you can wallow in the great what might have been.'

'I always knew it was mine,' he said solemnly. 'Was it a boy or a girl?'

'I don't want to talk about it. I'll wait till my tranquillizers start working.'

'Why are you taking tranquillizers?'

'To calm me down.

'You're upset, aren't you?'

She said nothing. He handed her the package and she opened it with neutral interest. It was a framed studio photograph of himself in racing gear.

'I've been asked to drive for the Bristol team at Le Mans this year,' he announced with pride.

'Is that good?'

'It means I've hit the jackpot as a driver.' He pointed to the photograph. 'That's the official team photo. I got one for you and one for my mother.'

Ruth got up to stand it on the dresser beside the pictures of Andrea and Georgina. She seemed low and preoccupied. David tried to cheer her up by giving her an invitation.

'You should've seen their faces at home when I told them! All of a sudden they've taken me seriously.' He moved closer. 'You've got to come to France with me. After the race we can have a holiday.'

'France?' There was a flicker of interest.

'You've never been abroad, have you?'

'I could learn French,' she mused. 'Take lessons . . .'

'We could go to Paris.'

'Yes . . . What will you do with The Emperor?'

'It's not important now,' he said, dismissively. 'We can probably sell her for scrap. We haven't got the money to repair her.'

'How much would you need?'

'Lots.'

'How much?'

'Ant reckons about £400.'

She shrugged. 'You ought to try to find it somehow. Be a shame to get rid of The Emperor after all the work you put into it. There must be someone who could give you the money.'

An idea nudged him. 'What about Desmond?'

'Desmond?'

'He's got plenty of money. Do you think he'd help?'

'Ask him.'

'I don't suppose you would?' Her expression gave him his answer. 'No, I thought not. Right. We'll go out and celebrate tonight. I'll pick you up at eight . . .'

The door opened and Andrea walked in.

'Hello,' said David, brightly.

'Hello.' It was a cautious reply.

'How's school?'

'It's nice.'

'Here's an Easter Egg,' said David, handing it to him. 'But you mustn't eat it till Sunday.'

'Okay,' agreed the boy, gratefully.

'Would you like to go to the Fair on Hampstead Heath tomorrow afternoon?'

'Yes please! What time?'

'Half-past three.'

'Half-past three,' echoed Andrea.

David turned to Ruth. 'I'll pick you up later tonight.'

He kissed her goodbye and went out.

Ruth picked up the photograph and read once more the inscription across the bottom of it.

'To Ruth,
With all my love,
David.'

It was a start.

9

They had lunch together at Goodwood Court and then all three of them went to the cinema. Ruth saw little of the film. Her mind was on David Blakely and she was once more finding excuses for his bad behaviour and trying to exonerate him. David had been upset about The Emperor. The tragedy during the race at Oulton Park had been such a blow to his pride and morale that he had not known what he was saying. His neglect of her after the miscarriage could be put down to trepidation. He was afraid to face her after his explosive attack on her at the racing circuit. Also, he had been deeply shocked by the news that they had lost their child and he had needed time to come to terms with it. Ruth clung to the fact that he had not wanted her to have an abortion. He had accepted the child as his.

'Can I have an ice cream, please?'

Andy's voice brought her out of her reverie and she saw that it was the intermission. She opened her purse to fumble for money.

'Take this,' said Desmond, giving the boy a pound note.

Andrea went off happily to buy three Walls ice creams.

'You spoil us, Des,' she said, squeezing his hand.

'Did you enjoy the film?'

'It was smashing.'

She saw even less of the second feature. David's face again appeared on the screen to occupy her attention and she read his message of love written underneath. Everything had changed now. In selecting him to drive at Le Mans, the Cooper-Bristol management had transformed her life. Their future together was now assured. Success for David as a racing driver. A holiday in France. Marriage. Bliss.

Ruth did not even remember the names of the two films.

When Desmond drove them back to Egerton Gardens, he was not invited in. Ruth was anxious to put her son to bed early. She had a bath, selected her favourite dress, then took extra care with her make-up. At her neck she wore the silver crucifix that he had given her. On her feet were black patent leather high-heeled shoes. Ruth felt happy and well for the first time since the miscarriage.

David's photograph stood on the dresser. David's bouquet of red carnations were in a vase on the table. She sat down and waited for the sound of his tread outside the door.

Eight o'clock came and went but there was no sign of him. An hour later, she was on her third glass of Pernod, still confident that he would come. By 9.30 P.M. that confidence had been supplanted by fear. David had had an accident in the car. Drink had finally caught up with him. He was lying in pain somewhere.

Ruth went down to the telephone in the entrance hall and rang the Findlaters. She persuaded herself that David might have got so drunk that he had stayed at Tanza Road. The au pair girl answered. Her grasp on the English language was not a strong one.

'I am here alone . . .'

'Has Mr Blakely *been* there? Do you know where he's gone?'

'Here is nobody else. Francesca, I look after . . .'

Going back upstairs to her bedsitter, Ruth poured out more Pernod and mixed it with recrimination. She paced up and down, smoking one cigarette after another, getting less and less reassurance from the photograph and the red carnations. Tucked up in the camp bed, Andrea slept through it all.

When she rang again at 10.30 P.M., Anthony Findlater answered.

'David was here, Ruth, but he went out.'

'When?'

'Hours ago.'

'Where?'

'He didn't say.'

'I was expecting him here.'

'He didn't mention it.'

'You must have *some* idea where he is.'

'Sorry, Ruth . . .'

There was an almost cocky note in his voice that served to inflame her suspicions. David *was* at Tanza Road. In her rage, she felt the Findlaters had persuaded him to keep away from her and to forget all about his promise of marriage. He was in hiding.

She rang Goodwood Court but Desmond was not there. After yet another drink, she rang Tanza Road once more. Anthony repeated what he had told her earlier. The pattern for the next hour or so had been set. Fruitless calls to Desmond. Additional calls to Tanza Road. More drink. More anger. More frustration. More pain.

After midnight, she finally got through to Desmond.

David Blakely sat on the edge of the sofa with his hands clasped tightly together. Ruth's repeated telephone calls had unnerved him. Carole had assured him that if Ruth arrived to create a scene then she and Anthony would handle her. David was safe. He could relax.

When the telephone stopped ringing, Carole decided that Ruth had given up. She took a sleeping pill, kissed David good night, and went off to bed. The au pair had already retired. The men were left alone together. Anthony made them a milky drink.

'I'm scared,' confessed David.

'She finally got the message. She won't bother you again.'

'You don't know, Ruth.'

'I know all I want to know.'

'She's capable of anything, Ant.'

'Leave her to us . . .'

To ease David's apprehension, Anthony got him talking about motor racing and they were soon lost in the technicalities of how best to cope with the circuit at Le Mans. David was slowly unwinding, showing interest, making plans, savouring his success.

Then they heard the car arrive down below in the street.

David was at the window in a flash.

'Cussens has brought her!'

'We won't let her in.'

'There she is!'

'We won't even answer the door.'

He pulled David from the window and they sat down.

The doorbell rang and rang with deafening persistence but they stayed where they were. At length it stopped and the car drove away. Ruth had gone. David's relief was short-lived. The telephone assaulted their ears again. Anthony picked up the receiver but put it down without speaking when he heard Ruth's voice.

'That's it now, David. She's tried everything.'

'Ruth won't give up.'

'She'll have to.'

But Ruth herself would not admit defeat. Coming out of the telephone kiosk, she made Desmond drive her back up Parliament Hill to Tanza Road. The doorbell came in for more punishment.

When it became clear that the door would remain shut, Ruth was boiling with exasperation. She ran down the ten stone steps and went over to David's Vanguard at the kerb. Watched by the impassive Desmond Cussen, she began to vent her fury on the car, abusing it, kicking it, beating it with her fists. She pulled off a shoe and used the heel to tap viciously against a window, splintering the glass until it formed an ugly cobweb. When she attacked the windscreen in the same way, Desmond came alive and leapt out of the Zephyr to dash over and restrain her.

'This has gone far enough!'

'I'm entitled to smash this thing up!' she maintained. 'I paid for half of it!'

'Do you want to get arrested?'

'Go home, Desmond . . .'

'Not without you. Now for Christ's sake stop making a fool of yourself, Ruth!'

Light suddenly spilled out from the window above them. A curtain had been drawn back in the Findlaters' flat and two figures were standing there and looking down. When Ruth swung round, the curtain was suddenly closed again and the light killed. She waved a fist.

'I know you're in there, David!'

'Ruth, please . . .' counselled Desmond.

'Come on out, you spineless coward!'

'There'll be trouble . . .'

'Is the au pair dropping her drawers for you again tonight, David?' she jeered. 'Is she panting in the bedroom for you! Does she know about *me*? Or that bloody mistress of yours in Penn? Or your sodding usherette? Has she realized the sort of bastard you are!'

She was still ranting when the police car arrived.

The two policemen tried to calm her down. One of them assessed the damage to the car and the other spoke to Desmond. It was a familiar problem for the local constabulary. They had seen it all before.

'I don't want to run her in if it's a lovers' tiff, sir.'

'I'll get her home,' promised Desmond.

'Did you damage this vehicle, madam?' asked the second policeman.

'I'm entitled to! I paid for half of it.'

Desmond put an arm around her. 'Come on, Ruth. It isn't worth it. Think about Andy.'

'Who's Andy?' asked the first uniform. 'The boy-friend.'

'Her son.'

'Yes,' she agreed, suddenly calm. 'My son . . .'

'I'll take her home . . .'

'Straight home, sir,' cautioned the first policeman.

Ruth's fury had spent itself for the moment. She was gazing up at the window of the Findlaters' flat in silence.

'She's all right now,' decided Desmond.

'Calmed down, madam?' checked the second police-man.

'Yes.'

'Good,' he said. 'I wouldn't like to run you in over the Easter holidays . . .'

Desmond gave the men a tired smile then escorted Ruth to his car. The policemen studied the damaged Vanguard again and then exchanged an amused look. It was another anecdote for the canteen back at the police station.

Tucked up under a blanket of cigarette smoke, Andrea slept peacefully on the camp bed. His mother, still dressed, still in pain, still unable to cope with David's betrayal, brooded in a chair and smoked incessantly. The injustice of it all rankled. She had given David her love and he had rejected her in the cruellest way. For longer than she could remember, she had abased herself for him. She had met his demands, coped with his depres-sions, put up with his tantrums, suffered his infidelities, and felt his violence. After all kinds of shameful behavi-our, she had wiped up his mess. The price had been high. It had cost her a job, her friends, her pride, her unborn baby. Ruth was now coming to fear that it would cost her sanity as well.

She picked up his photograph, looked at it for one last time, then put it away in a drawer. She lit another cigarette.

Desmond Cussen was still in his pyjamas when she arrived. He did not need to be told that she had passed a sleepless night. Ruth looked ill with fatigue. Yet there was a strange animation about her, a nervous energy that seemed to fuel her and keep her going even beyond the boundaries of exhaustion.

Her eyes were glistening with triumph.

'I saw him! He *was* there!'

'Where?'

'Tanza Road.'

'You've been back?'

'First thing this morning. I caught a cab then hid in the doorway opposite. David came out with Ant. They checked the Vanguard then drove off . . .'

'Ruth, this is ridiculous,' he argued.

'I proved it. He was there last night. In hiding.'

'Okay, he was there. Why not leave it at that?'

'Because I have to catch him.'

Desmond let out a moan of despair.

'And I know where he is,' she laughed. 'I worked it out.'

'Forget Blakely,' he urged. 'You're better off without him.'

But Ruth was in a world of her own. 'The car, you see. They couldn't drive round in it with the windows smashed like that so they had to be going somewhere to get it repaired. And I guessed which garage it was!' She was delighted at her detective work. 'They'd have no money, probably, so it would have to be a garage where they could put the charge on account. Clive Gunnell's place. Mayfair. I gave them long enough to get over there and then I rang from a call box . . .'

'What ever for?'

'I knew that David wouldn't speak to me so I gave a false name and asked for Ant. When he came on the line, I put on this sweet voice and said, "I just wanted to thank you for calling the fucking police last fucking night . . ." He hung up on me.'

'I don't blame him . . .'

'Now *you've* got to ring the garage, Des!'

'Why?'

'To find out if they're still there.'

'Ruth . . .'

'Hurry up. We don't want to miss them.'

'Look, I'm not getting involved in this stupid game!'

Five minutes later, he did as she asked.

Disguising his voice, he rang the garage to speak to Anthony and gave a false name. Anthony came on the line, heard two words, then hung up. Now that they had established that David and Anthony were still there, Ruth badgered Desmond into getting dressed then driving her across to Rex Place. They were too late.

Repairs to the Vanguard were completed. It had gone.

'They must have gone back to Tanza Road!' decided Ruth.

'We are not going back there now!' he insisted.

'I want to.'

'Isn't it time you thought about Andy?'

'Andy?' She had never heard the name before.

'Your son, Ruth. Left alone in the flat while you go charging off across London. The kid must be worrying himself sick.'

Under pressure from Desmond and pricked by conscience, she agreed to go back to Egerton Gardens to take care of Andrea. The three of them had lunch together and then Desmond suggested a visit to Regent's Park Zoo.

The boy loved the place and ran from cage to cage with excited interest. Desmond was surprised how much he himself enjoyed seeing the animals but his enjoyment was soon curtailed. Pointing out that Hampstead was only ten minutes away in the car, Ruth bullied and pestered until he agreed to take her. Andrea was given money to make his own way back home and the adults walked off.

Hampstead was busy. Traffic held them up.

Then they spotted the Vanguard.

It was parked outside the Magdala public house. Since it was almost closing time, David would soon be coming out so Ruth decided to wait for him near the Findlaters' flat. Desmond dropped her there.

'They mustn't see your car, Des.'

'What am I supposed to do?' he sighed.

'Cruise round . . .'

When Desmond left, she noticed that a house opposite was up for sale and that it was being decorated. Pretending to be a prospective buyer, she went over to size the place up and hide there until the Vanguard returned.

One of the plasterers saw her come in.

'Thinking of buying it, Blondie?'

'I might.'

'All the artists live round here.' He gave a crude laugh. 'Piss artists, most of them . . . Like a cup of tea?'

'No thanks.'

She lurked in the doorway long enough to see David and Anthony return, go into the house, then re-emerge with Carole, Francesca and the au pair, a plump teenage girl. David was laughing as he said something to the au pair and she giggled.

Jealousy pushed its knife even further into Ruth.

She watched the Vanguard take its five passengers left into Parliament Hill then she started walking. Certain that David was having an affair with the foreign girl, she decided that it had been set up by the Findlaters as a means of luring him away from her. Ruth had such a low opinion of Carole and Anthony that she could believe anything of them.

The Zephyr pulled up beside her.

'Come on, Ruth. Get in.'

'Okay.'

'We've seen enough of Magdala Road for one day.'

It was wishful thinking. Desmond was back that evening.

After giving Andrea his tea and putting him to bed, Ruth had demanded to be driven to Hampstead again. Her third visit of the day was no more reassuring than the others. A party was in progress at the Findlaters' flat. Music and laughter floated down. Then someone opened the window to let in fresh air. Ruth was certain that she heard David's voice and the au pair's distinctive giggle.

Not long afterwards, David, Anthony and the girl came out of the flat and made for the Vanguard. Ruth again heard David's voice.

'Let me put my arm around you for support . . .'

He passed within feet of Ruth's hiding place when he spoke. The girl gave an acquiescent laugh. The trio got into the Vanguard and pulled away. Ruth stumbled off down the road in a daze.

Desmond caught up with her.

'Your chauffeur, madam . . .'

She kept walking. 'It's the au pair. I was right.'

'I'm taking you home. Andy can't be left on his own.'

'No.' She got into the car and he drove off. That vile pig, David Blakely, promised to take him to the Fair. Andy will feel let down. Just like his mother!'

'You're tired. You need sleep.'

'How did I get here?'

'I brought you. And left you.'

'Thanks.'

'What happened?'

'There was a party going on.'

'Where were you?'

'In the road. Watching.'

'Don't you realize it's gone midnight, Ruth?'

'I know it's the au pair! They pulled the blind down in her room.'

'What does it matter?'

'He's up to his old tricks.

Desmond sighed. 'You'd still have him back.'

'I know,' she said.

The Fair had transformed Hampstead Heath into a world of coloured lights and concerted merriment. Dodgems crashed, chairoplanes whirled, roundabouts span, painted horses galloped, swingboats rose and fell, and the giant Ferris wheel explored the sky with fragile grace. Fine weather and the prospect of fun brought the holiday crowds out in abundance on Easter Sunday afternoon. Motors rumbled, girls screamed, barkers shouted, children laughed and a hundred other sounds contributed freely to the general fairground hustle and bustle.

David Blakely picked his way through the frothing hordes with Francesca Findlater on his shoulders. Carole and Anthony were with him and the au pair tagged behind. Ostensibly there for the child's benefit, they could not resist a go on the rifle range and the coconut shy and the Guess Your Weight machine. After his problems in recent weeks, David found it the perfect place to take him out of himself. He was happy, relaxed, amused and engrossed.

He did not realize that he was under surveillance.

Trailing him every inch of the way was Ruth Ellis.

The kitchen at Goodwood Court was small but superbly equipped. It had a new refrigerator of almost American dimensions but it was nearly empty. When a disgruntled Desmond Cussen opened the door, only a few bottles of tonic water and an ice tray were on duty. He scowled, took the ice tray to a work top, and started hammering the cubes to release them into a water jug. From the living room came the sound of a children's programme on television and he banged all the harder in order to block it out.

When the iced water was ready, he took it into the living room and set it down on the table beside a half-empty bottle of Pernod. Ruth was watching the television with the glazed expression of a dead salmon. Both she and Desmond were drinking Pernod as if it were orange squash on a blistering hot day.

Andrea was riveted to the screen.

Desmond sat down again and glared at the television with frank malevolence. When he could stand no more, he leapt to his feet and turned the machine off.

'That's enough! I'm sick of hearing it!'

Andrea was shocked and frightened. Ruth came awake.

'Go and play, Andy.'

'Where?'

'Anywhere!' howled Desmond.

Andrea quickly gathered up his comics and the remains of his chocolate Easter egg and scurried off to the study. From behind its door he could hear the adults clearly in the other room.

'I've had enough.'

'There was no need to upset him.'

'Being upset's nothing new to Andy.'

'It's bad enough David letting him down today without you turning on him.'

Desmond bridled. 'Oh, so now I'm as rotten as Blakely!'

'Of course not.'

'Oh, but I am, Ruth,' he said, darkly. 'I could be a damn sight worse than both of you put together if I let myself. You'd think more of me then.'

'No.'

'Yes! Yes!' he yelled. 'If I treated you like a punchbag instead of a woman, you might have thought the baby you've lost was mine and not Blakely's . . .' He grabbed hold of her. 'It could have been mine!'

'You're hurting me.'

'It could have been!'

'Desmond . . .'

'Say it!'

'Yes. It could,' she admitted, finally.

He released her but continued to stare down at her.

Ruth lifted her glass and drained it dry. Then she lay back on the sofa, closed her eyes and tried to shut out some of the ugliness of her life. Her tone was bitter and hopeless.

'How did I get involved with that disgusting little shit?' she asked herself. 'I didn't like him the first time I saw him. He lounged at the bar like little Lord Fauntleroy, peering down his nose at me and everybody else as though we were things he'd normally only expect to find at the bottom of a dung heap. I thought he was a pompous little pipsqueak.' She shook her head ruefully. 'If I had all the money he's borrowed or cadged off me, I'd be a rich woman! It's always the same. Every bloody man I've taken seriously turns out to be either a womanizer, a wife beater or a wino . . .'

'Which am I?' he asked, quietly.

She opened her eyes but kept them on the ceiling.

Desmond put down his glass, came to sit beside her, and gradually slipped his arms right around her. Ruth could do nothing to stop him as his hands felt for the zip on her dress and his tongue began to lick her face. He groped and twisted and pulled at her clothes then tore at his own. She was forced back at an uncomfortable angle but raised no word of protest as he grunted his way into her. The pent-up emotions and frustrations of his whole friendship with her came rushing out. Desmond had acted as her chauffeur and errand boy for long enough while she chased another man.

Now it was his turn.

Afterwards, panting, sweating, torn between guilt and triumph, he sat up and poured them both a drink. She swallowed hers gratefully. He looked at her as if waiting for words of approval or reproach.

But Ruth was not even thinking of him.

'I'm going back there . . .'

'For God's sake!' he protested.

'I've got to have it out with him, Des, don't you see that? I can't just let him get away with it.'

He was adamant. 'Don't expect me to take you.'

'I'll find a cab.'

'Stay away from him.'

'I can't.'

'But it's all so pointless!'

'Not to me!' Her features were contorted. 'I hate him for what he did. I hate David Blakely. He's got to be punished!'

He scrutinized her for some minutes.

'What would you do if you had Blakely here now?'

'I'd kill him,' she said, dully.

Desmond nodded grimly. Ruth had entered a realm of private grief beyond his reach.

It was early evening at the flat in Tanza Road. Francesca had been put to bed and the au pair was washing up the tea things. Carole was tidying the living room perfunctorily. The men lolled.

The telephone rang. David stiffened at once.

'It's her!'

'We don't know that,' said Carole.

'It could be Clive,' added her husband. 'He said he'd give us a call when he was ready to be picked up.'

'It's her!' insisted David. 'I know it!'

'Answer it,' decided Carole.

After some hesitation, he picked up the receiver.

'Hello . . .?'

Ruth's voice almost burst his eardrum.

'I hope you're having an enjoyable bloody holiday because you've ruined mine!'

Without waiting to hear any more, he slammed the receiver down. David was immediately on his feet in a welter of anxiety, pulling out a packet of cigarettes. He lit one and inhaled deeply.

'She can't touch you as long as you're here,' said Carole.

'I can't stay with you for ever!'

'She'll soon get fed up with hounding you,' decided Anthony.

'Not Ruth!'

'Then you'll just have to stand up to her and tell her to sod off!' rejoined his friend.

'You should have done that a year ago,' noted Carole.

'If only it was that easy!' sighed David. 'Awful thing is . . .'

'Go on,' urged Anthony.

'Part of me still wants her.'

'That would be fatal!' exclaimed Carole. 'After all that's happened, you *still* can't see the sort of person she is!'

'Did you really want to marry that?' asked Anthony.

'Yes.' He considered. 'Well, I thought so at the time.'

'And now?'

'I can see that it would be a mistake.'

'That's the Understatement of the Year!' sneered Carole. 'How could you ever *think* of it, David? You'd be throwing yourself away. She's a divorced woman with two children by different fathers. What sort of stability could you expect with a person like that?'

'None, I suppose . . .'

'Then don't weaken,' she warned. 'It's over. For good!'

David nodded in agreement. 'You've been wonderful to me this weekend. I owe both of you a great big thank you.'

'We're only too glad to help,' said Anthony.

'As long as you let us, that is,' added Carole.

David sat down again and puffed reflectively on his cigarette.

'Do you remember how we first met?'

'The Alfa Romeo!' recalled Anthony with a laugh.

'That thing!' sighed Carole. 'Biggest mistake I ever made was to buy you that car, Ant.'

'It was a beauty!' he argued.

'That was the trouble. It was more of a beauty to you than your wife was.' She stilled his protest with a raised palm. 'It was, Ant, and you know it. I gained a car and lost a husband.'

'But you also gained a friend through that car,' reminded David.

Fondly, Anthony cast his mind back.

'Yes! When we tried to sell the Alfa, you showed up with a pal of yours to check it over for him. We got talking cars . . .'

'And the pair of you are still at it!' complained Carole.

The men laughed then the telephone rang again.

This time Carole took charge.

'Hello . . .?'

'Carole? Clive here . . .'

She relaxed visibly. Clive was coming around for the evening with his record-player so that they could all have a quiet drink listening to music. He needed to be picked up and had rung to say that he was now ready. Carole replaced the receiver.

'Nip off and fetch him, David,' said Anthony.

'I'd rather not go on my own, if you don't mind.'

'Then I'll come with you,' volunteered Carole.

'What if she's out there?' he said, anxiously.

'You're safe with me,' she said and pushed him towards the door.

They left the flat and drove in the Vanguard to Mayfair, where Clive Gunnell was waiting to load his equipment into the boot. When they got back to the flat, David felt much more secure than when they left. He did not glance furtively around this time or fear that Ruth was going to jump out at him.

Drinks were poured, records selected, cigarettes lit. In a warm, congenial atmosphere, the four of them chatted amiably while the music formed an agreeable background. The talk, inevitably, turned back to The Emperor.

'We tried to race her too soon, that's all,' said Ant.

'What a let-down!' recalled Clive.

'Don't tell me,' protested David. 'I thought I'd die when the engine blew up on me. That was a day I'd rather forget!'

'Carole is the only one who got anything out of it,' noted her husband. 'She wrote a fashion article for the paper. You know – what the ladies wear to a big motor racing event.'

'I'm glad someone salvaged something out of Oulton Park,' said David. 'I certainly didn't.'

Carole opened a packet to take out another cigarette.

'I'm out of fags.'

'Have one of mine,' offered David.

'I'll need some more of my own,' she insisted. 'I must have a fag between my fingers.'

'We'll go to the pub and get you some,' volunteered Clive.

'Yes,' added David, 'and we'll get some more booze as well.'

The two men got up and sauntered towards the door.

'Don't be long,' warned Carole. 'I know what you two are like when you get inside a pub together.'

'We'll be back in no time at all,' promised David.

They descended the stairs and went out into the road.

'Shall we walk?' suggested Clive.

'The car will be quicker. Hop in.'

It was a decision that would turn out to be fatal.

Ruth Ellis sat in the back of a taxi and smouldered with resentment. One thought dominated her mind. David Blakely had betrayed her. He had invited her out and never shown up. He had offered to take her to France and never intended to do it. He had promised to marry her then cast her aside. Ruth had made enormous sacrifices on his behalf and he had taken them for granted. She felt that she had been used and discarded. David had deprived her of her self-respect. And now he had betrayed Andrea too. In failing to return and take the boy to the fair, David had finally pushed Ruth beyond the grip of self-delusion and desire.

Nothing that he could do would earn her forgiveness. She did not want his whining apologies any more. She did not want his red carnations. She did not want his empty promises.

Ruth simply wanted revenge.

When the taxi turned into Tanza Road and approached number 29, she slipped on her glasses to search for the Vanguard. It was not there. There was a light in the Findlaters' window and she knew from her earlier telephone call that they were in. David must have gone to the Magdala for drink or cigarettes. She ordered the cabbie to drive on to the pub.

Her instinct had been right. The Vanguard stood outside the entrance to the Magdala. It was parked on the bend and rested at an angle on the gradient. She stopped the taxi and got out.

Ruth kept on her glasses and peered through the stained glass window of the pub to see David Blakely and

Clive Gunnell drinking at the bar. Beside them on the counter were the three quart bottles of light ale and the cigarettes that they had just bought. David was asking something of the landlord who was giving an obliging smile by way of reply. Ruth saw David take out a cheque book and write in it. The landlord took five pounds from the till to cash the cheque.

Though she was tense, nervous and aching with tiredness, Ruth's resolve did not falter. As she watched David, she was reminded of all the pain and suffering he had caused her in the time that she had known him. And loved him. Her palm felt the side of her handbag. She was ready.

The men finished their drinks, gathered up their purchases, and came out through the door. They did not see Ruth pressed against the wall of the pub. Because the passenger door was locked, Clive had to wait to be admitted from inside. With a quart bottle tucked under his arm, David Blakely searched for a key that he would never use. Ruth stepped forward.

'David!' she hissed.

He ignored her and went to open the door.

She took a gun from her handbag and pointed it at him.

'David!' she called out.

He swung round, saw her, panicked, then ran to seek the protection of his friend on the passenger side of the car. Ruth fired two shots. As he was hit, David screamed only one word.

'Clive!'

Ruth pursued him around the car.

'Get out of the way, Clive!' she ordered.

The wounded David, crouching behind his friend, tried to flee.

Ruth fired again. He slumped in agony against the bonnet of the car and dropped the bottle to the ground with a crash. Her fourth shot cut him down and she stood over the twitching body to pump one more bullet into him.

David Blakely lay dying in a pool of blood.

Ruth now lifted the gun to her head and put the end of the barrel against her temple, but her finger would not pull the trigger. Losing her nerve, she lowered the gun and fired the last shot at the pavement. It ricocheted off the stone and hit the hand of a woman who had been passing by. More blood flowed.

Shuddering all over, Ruth Ellis now turned to Clive.

'Go and call the police,' she said.

Epilogue

At Hampstead Police Station, Ruth Ellis was charged with the murder of David Blakely and formally cautioned. Later the same day, she appeared at a special sitting of the Hampstead Magistrates' Court and was remanded in custody until April 20th to Holloway Prison. When she asked for a Bible and a photograph of David, both requests were granted.

Only forty-eight hours after the shooting, Ruth wrote a letter on prison notepaper to David's mother.

> 9656 Ellis
> H.M. Prison, Holloway N.7.
> 12.4.55.
>
> Dear Mrs Cook,
> No dought these last few days have been a shock for you. Please try to believe me, when I say, how deeply sorry I am to have caused this unpleasantness. No dought you will hear all kinds of stories, regarding David and I. Please do forgive him for deceiving you, has regarding myself. David and I have spent many happy times together . . .

She went on to talk about David and the events of that fateful 7th April, and about the bitterness she felt towards the Findlaters. She concluded by saying:

> Please excuse my writing but this pen is shocking. I implore you to try to forgive David for living with me, but we were very much in love with one and other unfortunately David was not satisfied with one woman in his life.
> I have forgiven David, I only wish I could have found it in my heart to have forgiven when he was alive.
> Once again, I say I am sorry to have caused you this misery and heartache. I shall die loving your son. And you should feel content that his death has been repaid.
> Goodbye
> Ruth Ellis

The trial began on June 20th, 1955 before Mr Justice Havers in Number One Court at the Old Bailey. Mr Christmas Humphreys led the prosecution and Mr Melford Stevenson appeared for the defence. Ruth was determined to be at her best in court. Three days before the trial the Governor of Holloway Prison allowed her access to hair-dressing materials and a wardress helped to dye her hair. When she arrived at the Old Bailey, she wore a black suit with fur trimmings and her face, framed under her striking platinum hair, was relaxed and smiling. She did not convey the impression of being contrite or guilt-stricken.

The trial lasted only two days. The jury needed no more than twenty-three minutes to reach the verdict of 'Guilty' with no recommendation of mercy. As the judge donned the black cap to pronounce sentence, Ruth bowed her head slightly.

The dull monotone echoed around the court.

'Ruth Ellis, the jury have convicted you of murder. In my view, it was the only possible verdict. The sentence of the court upon you is that you be taken hence to a lawful prison, and thence to a place of execution, and that you there be hanged by the neck until you be dead, and that the body be buried within the precincts of the prison within which you shall last have been confined before your execution, and may the Lord have mercy on your soul.'

The fragile figure in the dock remained calm. She smiled across at her parents and friends in the court and she brushed away the hands of the two wardresses who tried to help her below to the cells. She preferred to make her own way down the steps that would lead her out of the real world. A prison van took her back to Holloway to await her execution.

Resignation hardened her features during the last few weeks of her life. To pass the time she made stuffed toys with materials brought in by her mother or pieced together jigsaw puzzles. To gain comfort, she read the Bible. Relatives and friends visited her every day. If they tried to lift her spirits with news of the campaign to secure her reprieve. Ruth told them bluntly that she deserved to die. She had shot David Blakely with a Smith and Wesson revolver and put four bullets into the man she had loved. She sought no excuse.

'I have done this thing, I must die for it.'

At 9 A.M. on July 13th, 1955, Ruth Ellis was hanged at Holloway Prison.